THIS WON'T HURT A BIT. . . .

I picked up the phone and listened to the receptionist's urgent question.

"No," I said. "He isn't here."

"He'll be in his own surgery," Endicott said.

"She says he isn't," I told him. "His next patient has just arrived, and he hasn't taken the previous one yet."

I began to feel a faint disquiet. Why hadn't Tyler Meredith come in to see what all the commotion was about? It was *his* new anaesthetic that was being tested, after all.

En bloc, we moved toward the interconnecting door below the level of the small intersecting X-ray room. Sir Malcolm took the doorknob with the same no-nonsense grip he might have used on a pair of forceps and swung the door open. "Wakey, wakey in there," he roared.

There was no response from the figure stretched out in the dental chair. As we advanced farther into the room, we could see the mask—like an oxygen mask—strapped over his face; hear the hissing of the tank hooked into the wheeled stand.

I didn't need to see the faint glitter of the partially open eyes to know that Tyler Meredith wasn't going to wake again.

Also by Marian Babson

IN THE
TEETH OF
ADVERSITY

Marian Babson

BANTAM BOOKS
NEW YORK · TORONTO · LONDON · SYDNEY · AUCKLAND

This edition contains the complete text
of the original hardcover edition.
NOT ONE WORD HAS BEEN OMITTED.

IN THE TEETH OF ADVERSITY

*A Bantam Crime Line Book / published by arrangement with
St. Martin's Press*

PUBLISHING HISTORY
St. Martin's edition published 1990
Bantam edition / July 1992

ISBN 0-553-29131-9

Published simultaneously in the United States and Canada

PRINTED IN THE UNITED STATES OF AMERICA

RAD   0 9 8 7 6 5 4 3 2 1

IN THE
TEETH
OF
ADVERSITY

Chapter 1

Simple things amuse simple minds. I was deriving quite a bit of amusement from the early edition of the evening paper. I had just made a note of the rapidly rising actress on page seven, who had been photographed against the background of her antique silver collection, holding the prize piece of carved jade from her treasury of objets d'art, and captioned by a melancholy quote saying how much she was going to miss her little mews cottage and her treasures during the next three months when she would be filming in

Spain. I underscored her name and made a nota-
tion to get in touch with her after the burglary,
when she would be looking for another—and
brighter—public relations person.

"Stop that!" I shouted as a bandit-masked whirl-
wind sprang from an ambush of late-afternoon shadows and hurled herself at my Biro. Capturing it
successfully, she tumbled over and over across the
desk, kicking at it with her hind legs and uttering
loud yowls of defiance.

You had to laugh at the little clown. A fact she
constantly used against me. "Behave yourself." I
tried to recapture the Biro, but she rolled away
from me with it, growling as though she really meant
it. Only the rakish tilt of her ears betrayed her play-
fulness.

"Come on, give it back." I feinted for it again,
and her tail lashed menacingly, her slanted blue eyes
glittering. She was having a lovely time.

"Be a good cat," I said. I had dropped the paper
by now and she had my full attention. Which was
what she'd wanted all along.

Suddenly, she abandoned the game. The Biro
dropped from her mouth and rolled across the desk
unnoticed. She was taut and alert, blue eyes staring
at the door. I followed her look, seeing nothing but
the closed door. After a moment, though, I heard it,
too.

Someone was taking the stairs two at a time.
Someone gained the tiny hallway and pounded on the
door, but didn't wait for any social niceties like being
invited to enter. He burst through the door, slamming
it behind him and leaning against it, looking around

wildly, gasping for breath. His eyes were bulging, his face purple, but he was just recognizable—the white coat helped.

I gazed at him in mild amazement. True, I was three or four months overdue for my semiannual checkup, but you don't really expect your dentist to get *emotional* over a fact like that. Particularly, as Gerry and I were practically the only National Health patients he had on his eminent and star-studded roster of Famous Mouths I Have Looked Into.

"You've got to help me," he choked. "You've got to help me, *now*. Quickly!"

It was a good line, and probably one he had picked up from patients ringing in the middle of the night with throbbing abscesses. But it seemed to be slightly misdirected.

"Are you sure you have the right place?" That was as near as I dared get to asking him if he knew where he was. "This is Perkins and Tate—"

"Public Relations, Limited," he finished for me. "Of course, it's the right place. Public relations—that's what I need right now. God! How I need public relations!"

It was a statement to warm the cockles of many a heart at the Institute of Public Relations, but it simply made *my* blood run cold. I mean, public relations isn't usually something you need immediately, like a fix, or a stiff drink. If you do, it means the horse has bolted, the barn has burned to the ground, the ground has caved into a previously unsuspected mineshaft, and somebody is handing you a rusty hasp and demanding that you put it all back the way it was.

Pandora glared at him, twitching her nose, then abruptly dived under the desk, hissing. She had recently had the last of her booster shots, and men in white jackets smelling, however faintly, of antiseptic were at the top of her Hate Parade.

He ignored her; I doubt that he even noticed her. He was still staring wildly in my general direction, waiting for me to wave the magic wand and make everything all right again.

"Why don't you sit down, and we'll talk this over," I suggested.

"Sit down? We haven't time! We've got to get into action now, you fool! Don't you understand? She's dead. Morgana Fane! She died under the anaesthetic in *my* dental chair. My God! *Morgana Fane!*"

I instantly needed a stiff drink myself. Morgana Fane—the Model of the Moment—of this decade. About to be the Bride of the Year. That mesmeric face, which had decorated a thousand magazine covers, launched a thousand styles, and—it was rumoured in the peephole press—shipwrecked a few dozen marriages, now stilled forever. It was the end of an Era.

Fortunately, the company was fairly solvent at the moment, and there was a bottle of Scotch in the kitchen cupboard. Going for it, I asked, "What did the police say about it?"

"I haven't called them!" He was affronted. "Not yet. That's why I came to you. I want a press representative with me before I do."

Oh, fine. At the rate he was going, a solicitor

would be more help when the police arrived. They were not going to take kindly to playing second fiddle to a public relations man. Although I appreciated the good dentist's problem. A society/show business practice, of the kind he had built up, depends on word-of-mouth recommendations and confidence. Lots of confidence. He could go out of style as fast as an old-fashioned abortionist if the death of a famous patient wasn't handled properly. Faster. And Morgana Fane—I found myself echoing the dentist—my God!

"Didn't she respond at all to the kiss of life?" I turned just in time to catch the shifty look that flashed across his face. He hadn't bothered to try. He'd been too worried about his own skin. He'd flown for a press representative—probably leaving her still there in the chair. *That* would look great in the headlines.

I took the drink I had poured for him and put it back in the cupboard beside the bottle—Gerry could drink it later. We were going to have enough problems without our dentist facing the music with liquor on his breath. It would be all the press needed—and I didn't think the police would react too favourably to it, either.

"There was no point in trying," he defended hastily, having evidently caught the look that flashed across *my* face just before I turned away. "Any fool could tell that she was gone."

There was a steady hissing sound emanating from beneath the desk. I just looked at him, my face as blank as I could possibly make it. I felt like joining Pandora under the desk for a hissing session, but it was a luxury I was denied.

This expensive dentist had not carried Perkins & Tate (Public Relations) Ltd. on his National Health books just because he could not resist our winsome faces. It was one of those tacit understandings, and Gerry and I had dutifully seen to it that his name was planted in a few columns and the discreet mention was inserted wherever possible. Very discreet—the dental profession being as twitchy as the medical on the subject of publicity. It had worked quite well and to our mutual satisfaction for several years. This time, however, the piper was really presenting the bill—and with a vengeance.

"She's still there," I said flatly. Just checking, I didn't expect any contradiction.

I didn't get one. "Right where she expired," he said. His face twitched with indignation. "In *my* dental chair!" He made it sound as though the only decent thing she could have done was to crawl into an anonymous gutter to die.

"What about your nurse?"

"She wasn't there today. Fortunately, she has the flu." It was obvious that he was grateful for a woman with some grasp of fundamental decencies.

"Does anyone know you've come here?" That was the first thing. If we could cover his tracks to Perkins & Tate, we might have a chance of retrieving the situation.

"I didn't tell anyone—if that's what you mean. And no one saw me leave the office."

That checked out. The reception and waiting rooms were on the ground floor, the torture chambers were upstairs. The front door opened into the hallway and faced the stairs; you had to detour through a door on the left into the reception area and the waiting room. The nurse notified you when your number had come up, and with a brave smile, you went through the door and up the stairs to whatever doom awaited you. The door was always closed, presumably so that the nervous clientele in the waiting room couldn't see the victims staggering out after they had been worked on.

Since Endicott Zayle hadn't had the bad luck to encounter someone actually entering as he was slipping out, he would not have been seen. If we could get him back in again without being seen, there might be a fighting chance.

"When did this happen?"

He seemed calmer, now that he had thrown the burden on someone else's shoulders. "About ten minutes ago."

That wasn't so bad. If he'd had to go and call in the wrong people, at least he hadn't let any grass grow under his feet about it. He didn't seem wholly aware of the enormity of what he had done, or how it would sound if the papers got hold of it. He was too concerned with the fact of her death to consider his own desertion of her.

"How did you get here?"

"I took a taxi."

He must have been fairly conspicuous in that white jacket. Could we take a chance that no taxi driver would remember? Even a doctor on the most urgent emergency call would throw on a coat before going out in weather like this. But taxi drivers, as a whole, are the most sophisticated social group in England, as well as the most discreet. With good reason—if they told all they knew, a few bastions of our society would crumble, and we don't have all that many left.

"You didn't do anything silly"—it was better to find out the worst right away—"like keeping the taxi waiting, did you?"

"Certainly not." He bristled. "I realize it wouldn't look too well if the police discovered I came to you before I called them."

It would look bloody awful, but I was relieved to find he had some inkling of the fact.

"Naturally, I've prepared a story in advance," he said. "In case they find out."

This cheered me a bit more. Perhaps he was brighter than he had previously given indication of being. "What story?" I asked hopefully.

"I shall say"—a crafty light glittered in the depths of his tiny eyes—"Everything Went Black. And when I came to, I was here." He waited triumphantly for my applause.

I looked at him bleakly. To get away with that one, you have to be 36-22-34 and preferably blond. At 44-52-58 and going bald, it just wasn't on. I tried to break it to him gently. "That one went out with 'I didn't know the gun was loaded.' "

He bristled, about to take umbrage again, when the steady hissing sound from under the desk unnerved him. "What's that?" He looked around uneasily. "Is something going to explode?"

"Only the cat," I said.

"Cat?" Locating the source of the sound, he crouched to look under the desk.

Lashing her tail, Pandora retreated, switching from a hiss to a growl. She knew his sort, she informed him. They petted you and chucked you under the chin and called you sweet names, and just when you were preening yourself that you'd made a new conquest, they jabbed a dirty great needle into your rump.

"I don't think she likes me," he said.

"She's shy," I said. "Don't worry about her." It seemed superfluous to tell him to worry about himself; it was amazing that anything could distract him from that absorbing concern.

He and Pandora continued staring at each other, which, ordinarily, would have been all right. However, it was wasting time, and back at the surgery, his partner, a restless patient, or even a just-recovered nurse might open the door to his office and discover the Corpse of the Year—with the dentist gone missing. Even the most loyal partner might be forgiven for jumping to conclusions under those circumstances—not to mention the police.

"Look," I said. "The best thing for you to do is get straight back to your surgery and call the police. Take my coat—you're pretty conspicuous in that white jacket—I'll pick it up later. I'll follow along right behind you. Then if the police question my presence, I'll say I had a sudden toothache and dropped in for emergency treatment." It might not be the best story in the world, but it was several cuts above his. And I might be able to knock together a better one between now and the time the question actually came up.

He didn't move.

"Hurry up," I urged. How long did it take a body to cool? Long enough for the police to detect the length of time between death and the time they were called in? "We haven't much time."

"I—I haven't told you everything—yet," he said. He seemed more interested in gazing into Pandora's eyes—however baleful—than in looking up and meeting mine. "You don't know the worst."

I usually don't. "Go ahead," I said grimly. "Surprise me."

"Morgana is—was—desperately afraid of hypodermics. I did everything to try to save that tooth— I've babied it along for years. But it was no use anymore. And she'd never had a tooth out before. The very thought made her hysterical. I assured her that the extraction was necessary, but she'd worked herself up into such a state—"

He still hadn't looked away from Pandora. She was working herself up into quite a state, too. "Go on," I said.

"Well, Tyler Meredith—my partner—has been developing a new anaesthetic. A gas type. He's worked on it for a long time, with very good results. We thought ... "

I began to see where this was leading, but I didn't want to believe it. I closed my eyes and hoped that, when I opened them again, the nightmare would have run its course.

It hadn't. He was still there, still staring into Pandora's eyes, still babbling on.

"... I can't understand it. We had such wonderful results with the laboratory animals—"

"Just let me get this straight," I interposed weakly. "You mean that you used *Morgana Fane* as a guinea pig for an untried anaesthetic?"

"No! No!" He quivered with shock and tore his eyes away from Pandora at last. "I told you we'd tested it on guinea pigs—*real* guinea pigs. The results were excellent. Economy of operation, foolproof administration, the patient went under immediately, knew nothing, recovered in a minimum of time, with no side effects—"

"Except that the patient died."

"She agreed." He was almost tearful.

"In writing?" I asked hopefully. Perhaps we could build her up as a willing martyr to science. A heroine, undergoing risks, so that others might never know the terror—

"No," he said reluctantly. "I never thought of that."

I stood there and wondered if a few tiny hunks of silver amalgam were worth it. But it was too late to give them back.

"Here." I crossed to the closet and took out my overcoat. "Put this on and get back to your surgery. You'll have to level with the police, but we ought to be able to work out a story for the newspapers later."

He hesitated. "Are you sure—?"

"Do we have a choice?"

He looked as though he'd thought of an answer to that one, too, but I didn't want to hear it. With his type of brain, it undoubtedly involved moving the body to some neutral ground and trying to pretend that she'd never kept her appointment. Judging from the speed with which he'd come running to Daddy, I didn't have any illusions about who had been cast as the corpse remover, while he stayed snug in his surgery establishing an alibi.

"Believe me, it's the only way," I said firmly, shoe-horning him into my coat. It was a snug fit, but it buttoned enough to hide the white jacket, which was the important thing.

"If you're positive . . . " He was still dragging his feet. I didn't exactly blame him. I wasn't too anxious to look on the last remains of Morgana Fane myself. A little of the zest goes out of living—even if only temporarily—when one of the legendary ones dies.

And Morgana Fane was as legendary as they come. Since she was discovered while performing in some quaint act at a remote seaside pier some fifteen years ago, she had been propelled into a fame which had never subsided. She was not only breathtakingly photogenic, she had a gift for getting into headline-dominating situations. The manner of her demise was going to be no exception. It wouldn't be easy, trying to soft-pedal this.

"I'll come downstairs with you." I took Zayle's arm, allowing him no escape. "And I'll be in the taxi right behind yours. All you have to do is get back upstairs to your own surgery without being seen. I'll go straight into the waiting room and you can leave the rest to me."

"But—" He was looking back over his shoulder at Pandora. "Will she be all right here by herself?"

Pandora arched her back and spat at him. She

was a cat prepared to sell her life dearly. If she had to go, she was going to take someone else with her.

"I think she prefers it," I said. "At any rate, my secretary is due in about half an hour."

Which reminded me. I went back to the desk, ignoring the nasty comments from underneath it, and scrawled a hasty message. "Gone to the dentist. Emergency. Expect me when you see me. Doug."

It was as close to the truth as it was wise to get on paper.

Chapter 2

You don't see people at their best in a dentist's waiting room. In fact, you don't see them at all. No one bothered to focus on me as I entered, and if my case had been as serious as I'd been representing to the receptionist in loud tones, I wouldn't have bothered noticing them either.

As it was, I had a good look round while I crossed to an empty chair. Three dulled faces looked up from glossy magazines, just checking to make sure I wasn't anyone who was going to call their names.

The fourth seemed actively annoyed that I

wasn't. "I've been here half an hour," he complained. "It's not like Malcolm to keep me waiting. Are you certain he knows I'm here?"

"Quite positive, Sir Geoffrey." The new receptionist, who had—unnecessarily—guided me into the waiting room, smiled brightly.

The old boy twirled his moustache and leered at her, betraying as fine a set of porcelain choppers as had ever been seen outside an antique shop. That explained why *he* wasn't afraid of seeing his dentist more than twice a year. Old Sir Malcolm—Endicott's father—determinedly fighting the spectre of retirement, listed his chess and poker pals as patients and scheduled them throughout the working day, so that he could maintain the fiction of still engaging in a busy practice in his top-floor office. It was relatively harmless, as self-deceptions went, and I knew the active partners encouraged him in it—if only to keep him out of their hair and their offices.

"Perhaps I ought to go up." Sir Geoffrey leaned forward, shifting his weight to his silver-knobbed walking stick preparatory to rising. "Malcolm may have forgotten me. It's a long time since you announced me."

"I'll remind him again." The receptionist had a steely note in her voice. "He *is* busy, you know." It was clear that she had no intention of allowing patients to roam about the premises as they pleased.

Which suited me. If there was any roaming to be done, I intended to be the one to do it, and it must be soon. By now, Zayle must have called the police and it would be beyond their comprehension if, having done so, he calmly rang downstairs for the next patient to be sent up so that he could fill in the time while waiting for their arrival. On the other hand, in the state he was in, it was just the sort of thing he might do. It was up to me to forestall him and get upstairs with him before the police came.

I gave a muffled groan and put a hand up to my jaw. I didn't even get a glance of sympathy from any of the others. Perhaps the groan had been too muffled—on my way out, I had snatched up a long scarf and wound it around my neck a couple of times. I felt that it not only gave the proper effect for someone suffering from a toothache, but it helped to disguise my identity.

Loosening the scarf enough to let sound escape it, I tried again. This time I gave a modified version of the anguished yowl Pandora lets out when she realizes that we are actually going past the fishmonger's without going in.

There were three short, sharp exclamations of sound as magazines hit the floor, having dropped from nerveless fingers. As befitted one who had seen action in numerous campaigns through the course of several wars, Sir Geoffrey was the first to leap into action.

"Good God, lad!" he cried. "Hold fast! Here—" He rapidly unscrewed the bulbous silver top from his walking stick and inverted the stick over it. The aroma of five-star Channel brandy filled the room as he thrust the bulb into my hand. "Here—drink this!"

I'd always suspected the cat of overacting. But I couldn't complain of inattention now. Every eye was

on me. There was nothing to do but sip the brandy
with what I hoped they'd take for a brave smile.

"That's the spirit, lad!" Sir Geoffrey encouraged. It certainly was—about 120 proof. He must
have had it smuggled in privately.

"Terribly sorry," I apologized. "My tooth . . . suddenly . . . emergency. But"—I shrugged deprecat-
ingly, looking around at them—"you were here first
. . . with appointments . . . I can wait"—visibly, I
controlled a wince—"until the dentist can fit me in."

As I had expected, it was the one queue in
which every true Englishman would gladly relinquish his place to another. The babble was deafening.

"Wouldn't hear of it." "Take my place—only a
check-up." "I can wait. Nothing urgent."

"Nonsense, lad!" Sir Geoffrey's voice overrode
them all. "You can come up with me. Sir Malcolm
himself will work on you."

I paled. Sir Malcolm's tactics in field hospitals
from the Somme to Salerno had figured largely in the
bittersweet reminiscences of famous military leaders.
To the point that it seemed probable, when future
historians began investigating certain famous
engagements in depth, they would discover an
appointment with Sir Malcolm in the morning had led
to more charges Over the Top than were motivated
by any desire to win glory for King and Country.

There might be nothing wrong with me when I
went into Sir Malcolm's surgery, but there would be
when I came out.

"Drink up," Sir Geoffrey urged, "and we'll be on
our way. Don't sip—gulp it down. That's prime stuff.
Why, I've seen amputations carried out in emer-

gency field theatres with no more than that used as anaesthetic."

I gulped. "No, really," I said, trying not to choke. "I couldn't do that. I mean, the *young* Zayle is my dentist. It would offend professional courtesy, or something, if I went to his father, wouldn't it?"

"Quite right," a no-nonsense female voice said firmly. "You must take my place. I must get back to the House, in any case. I can't wait here all afternoon."

I took another look at the lady. Now that the colour was creeping back into her face at the prospect of evading her appointment and the magazine no longer masked her, I recognized her as the Rt. Hon. Kate Halroyd, one of our more embattled lady MPs.

"Thank you," I said. "That's very kind of you."

"Not at all." She reinforced her words with a wide smile, and I could see that she had had plenty of practice in the past at avoiding dental appointments.

"You could take my appointment," the other woman said. She, too, was identifiable now: the Hon. Edytha Cale-Cunningham, more usually seen in the context of horse and paddock and race meets. "But mine is with Ty—Mr. Meredith. *He* seems to be taking quite a long while, too," she added wistfully.

"Perhaps they're in conference," I suggested. With Morgana Fane expired upon their premises, the partners had quite a lot to confer over. I only hoped that Zayle had started the due processes of the law rolling before he'd got sidetracked. The thought unnerved me so much that I winced in earnest.

"You mustn't stand here in agony, poor boy,"

the MP said as solicitously as though I'd been in her constituency. "Go straight up and tell Mr. Zayle that I said you were to have my appointment."

"Very kind of you," I said. "If you're quite sure—"

"And tell Morgana to hurry up." The other man hadn't spoken before. As he was the only nonentity in the room—besides myself—that meant that he must be the latest in the constant succession of Morgana Fane's business managers. "Tell her we're due at *Vogue* in half an hour."

I nodded. It wasn't for me to inform him that Morgana Fane was not receiving messages anymore. I wasn't supposed to know yet. I was just an innocent bystander who had dropped in for emergency treatment.

"Thanks," I said, handing the silver bulb back to Sir Geoffrey. "Thanks—all of you. I really appreciate this."

"Wait a minute, lad." Sir Geoffrey halted me as I started out. "Strategy—that's what we need. All very well for this lady to give up her appointment, but that receptionist has her own ideas. I've crossed swords with her more than once. Damned contrary wench. She'd never let you get past her desk. Tell you what, I'll engage her in conversation and you slip past when she isn't looking."

It seemed as good a plan as any; I was still cheered to know that access to the surgery was guarded so zealously. It reduced the chance of anyone's having wandered up to see what was taking so long. Not that I thought anyone had. They'd all been sitting around much too calmly for that. Morgana

Fane's was not a body one might stumble across lightly.

Voices rose heatedly in the reception area. I didn't need Sir Geoffrey's frantic signal, as the receptionist flounced over to a filing cabinet, to slide past and dive for the door.

The thick carpeting on the stairs would have muffled any sound, even if I hadn't been trying to be quiet. It wasn't just that I preferred to remain unnoticed by the receptionist, nor even that I felt it would be lacking respect to the recently departed to make noise. It was something else—a dark, breathless void about the atmosphere—as though the whole house were gathering itself together against the explosion which was to come.

I found Endicott Zayle hovering in the doorway of his tiny X-ray room between the surgeries. He was staring at the closed door of his own surgery with wide, haunted eyes, as though he were waiting for some spectre to emerge and begin haunting him for the rest of his life.

He might be right. Certainly, if we couldn't smooth this unhappy incident over, it would haunt him in the press and in his professional, if not private, life from now until retirement. It would even figure prominently in his obituary notice, the reminiscences of the event quite over-shadowing his own demise. Haunting enough for any man, with no help from the supernatural necessary.

"You've called the police," I said, trying to make it a statement and not a question.

He turned wild, glazed eyes onto me and I knew the answer.

"A doctor?"

"I—I can't. I couldn't use the telephone downstairs where everyone could hear me. Any my other telephone"—he gestured helplessly toward the closed door—"is in there. I—I can't go in there again."

I checked my watch. Incredibly, only a quarter of an hour had passed since we'd left my office. We still had time—if we didn't delay any longer. I started for that closed door.

"No, wait—" He grabbed my arm, holding me back. "Give me just another minute, to—to—"

"You've had plenty of time to get used to it," I said firmly, trying to shake him off. "The longer we delay now, the worse it will look."

"But you don't understand." He gripped tighter. "You can't. You're a layman. You only read about it in the papers from time to time. You can't know what it means to a professional. It's the nightmare we all dread. A patient—someone who looked and acted perfectly normal—sitting there, perfectly all right one moment. And the next—with no warning. You can never tell beforehand who's going to react in what way. Every patient is a bit apprehensive. It's too bad, but it's natural—from their point of view—I suppose. But *one* of them—one in perhaps hundreds of thousands—is going to be so abnormally terrified that there's a fantastic overproduction of adrenaline coursing into their bloodstream and—that's it. They die! Right there in your chair. They die of fright."

It was a good routine. I nodded, making mental notes for future use, wondering if he could reproduce just those same impassioned tones if he was called upon to do it again for the press. However, the press was one thing—and just between ourselves was another. Between ourselves, there were other things to be sorted out.

"Unless," I said ruthlessly, "they die because a new anaesthetic isn't all their dentist thought it would be."

For a moment, I thought his own adrenaline was going to come up with something pretty nasty. He went a mottled purple and began taking deep breaths.

However, he'd let go of my arm and I took advantage of the opportunity to fling open the door of his surgery.

Once that was done, it seemed to break the trance he was in and he entered slowly behind me. Everything looked much the same as it had on my last visit. The same sterilizing cabinet, the tray of instruments set out on the side table, the rack with the X rays of the day's patients. Everything looked exactly the same to my eyes.

Even the chair. Empty and waiting for me.

"This was a pretty sneaky trick to get me to keep an appointment." I turned to him accusingly. "Did Gerry think this one up for you?" There were times when I wouldn't put anything past my partner, and this was one of them.

"I don't understand . . ." His eyes bulged and his arms flapped feebly in protest against what he was seeing. "She was *here* —in that chair." He advanced upon the chair as though the body might come into focus if he got near enough.

"She isn't there now," I said, reinforcing the evidence of his own eyes.

"But—but where *is* she?" That adrenaline must have been doing a war dance through his system now. I hoped he wasn't going to expire upon my hands. "She can't have just disappeared. What's happened to her—her body?"

I looked around helpfully, but the room remained the same. It was shining and clean—sterile in fact. And completely nook-and-crannyless, the better to achieve the acme of sterility. There wasn't room to hide a small mouse, let along a full-grown female body.

I turned my look to Zayle with some suspicion. There wasn't even any gas apparatus in the room. Dentists, I suppose, are only human. They must have their pressures and tensions like the rest of us. It was just possible that he was cracking up. And it was typical of Perkins & Tate's luck that he should have chosen to have his nervous breakdown all over us.

"You're sure," I inquired delicately, "that—er—?"

"Of course, I'm sure," he snarled. "You don't think I could mistake something like that?"

"Not mistake, exactly," I said. "But—perhaps you've been overworking lately?"

It was the wrong thing to say, of course. But in a situation like this, it was hard to find the right thing.

"Are you suggesting"—he began advancing on me with a nasty look in his eyes—"that I'm imagining things?"

"No, no." I backed away hastily. He wasn't armed, but there were any number of sinister instruments lying on that tray, ready to be snatched up and wielded at a moment's provocation. "Certainly not. It—it was just a theory that sprang to mind. I can see how silly it was."

"You mean—" He was not about to be mollified. "You don't think I'm overworked. Possibly you don't believe I work at all?"

"No, no, you work very hard. I'm sure of it. I've seen you at work. You and your partner, both."

"Tyler—" His wild eyes turned toward the wall separating their surgeries. "Yes, Tyler. He might have come in to speak to me, taken in the situation, and—"

"And disposed of the body for you," I finished, without any great triumph. It was probably what had happened, which meant we were back where we started from, only in a worse mess than before. I'd have preferred the nervous breakdown. It was going to be even harder to present this to the press as a perfectly normal and understandable reaction than the original dereliction of duty.

The police, also, took a notoriously dim view of people's playing musical chairs with bodies—it looked like a suspiciously guilty reaction. And, I recalled, it was Tyler Meredith who had invented the new anaesthetic they were testing on Morgana Fane.

"Well." I looked at Endicott Zayle. Now that he had settled the question of the disappearance to what was apparently his own satisfaction, he seemed to have lost interest in it. He had stopped by the tray of instruments and was fiddling with them. "Hadn't we better go and ask him about it?"

"Oh, no, that's quite all right." Zayle continued to

potter happily with some sinister-looking probes and angled mirrors. "Tyler will have taken care of everything. We needn't bother anymore."

While I considered it laudable—in fact, necessary—to have every confidence in your partner, I still felt Zayle's attitude left something to be desired. Responsibility, perhaps. Not to mention a sense of duty, a conscience, a—

Looking beyond Zayle, at the doorway, I found my thoughts colliding like irresponsible motorists on a foggy M1. I tried to find my voice, and after a moment, I succeeded.

"You're sure," I said softly, "you're absolutely positive that Morgana Fane was really dead when you left her in that chair?"

"Of course, I am." He glared at me, bristling. "Don't you think I can recognize a cadaver when I see one? What kind of fool do you take me for?"

I smiled weakly, still looking beyond him. There wasn't much of an answer I could give to that one. Not with Morgana Fane standing in the doorway behind him.

Morgana Fane, alive and breathing. Breathing fire, in fact. She charged into the room, radiating fury.

"*There* you are!" she said. "What in hell is going on around here?"

Chapter 3

I was glad she'd asked the question. I was dying to know the answer myself.

Zayle stiffened as though he'd been shot in the back and turned slowly. "No," he said. "No!"

"Where did you *go*? Where have you *been*?" Morgana Fane whirled into the room, still on the attack. "I thought you were a reputable dentist, but you pump my lungs full of that disgusting stuff, and then you disappear for hours. I don't believe you care *that* much"—she snapped her fingers in his face—"for your patients. You're nothing but a quack!"

"Miss Fane." Zayle reeled backward. I stood by to catch him if he started to collapse, as seemed not unlikely. "My dear Miss Fane!"

"She's right, you know, m'boy." The gaunt gray figure, like the ghost of another era, followed Morgana Fane into the office. "Can't treat patients that way. Upsets 'em."

"Father!" Zayle turned his harassed eyes to the elderly man. "What are you doing here? You ought to—I mean, you have your own surgery. Upstairs. Your own patients. Shouldn't you be up there with them?"

"Found this poor little thing wandering around the top floor in distress," Sir Malcolm said indignantly. "Couldn't leave her roaming around on her own, could I? You were nowhere about. Took her in— I was between patients—and we've been playing chess. Clever little puss. Not a bad brain—for a woman. Might be something in giving them the vote, after all."

"I was looking for *you*," Morgana Fane said to Zayle. "You went off and left me all alone.

"It was absolutely frightful," she appealed to me. "There I was, lying back, unable to *move*, and he suddenly looked down at me with a frightening expression and bolted from the room. I thought something must have gone wrong and that I was dying.

"But it was like being underwater—I couldn't speak—I couldn't move—and I kept waiting for you to come back and help me. But you didn't." She faced Zayle accusingly. "I don't know what that stuff you had me inhaling *was*, but it was the most awful experience of my life."

"Always told you, m'boy, no good comes of mollycoddling patients. Anaesthetics—pah!" Sir Malcolm
snorted. "We never had time for mollycoddling at the
front. Plain and simple—that was the ticket. You put
your knee on the fella's chest, gave a few short,
sharp yanks and there you were. Neat as a pin.
Then your orderly brought 'im round and sent in the
next patient."

"Please, Father," Zayle said weakly, "why don't
you go back upstairs? It must be time for your next
patient."

"More than time," I put in helpfully, "he's downstairs. Sir Geoffrey, getting impatient. He thinks
you've forgotten about him."

I was all in favour of getting General Sir
Malcolm out of the way. We had enough trouble on
our hands. It wasn't the PR problem I'd been called
in to take care of, but it might be just as serious. If
Morgana Fane decided to sue for malpractice, or
something of the sort, she'd have quite a case.
Experimenting with a new anaesthetic—with
Morgana Fane as your guinea pig. I shuddered quietly. The idea alone was good for a long term at the
Scrubs. And when she turned those luminous green
eyes on the judge and jury, there'd be a fresh outcry
to bring back hanging. When I looked into those
eyes myself, I had understood for the first time why
men joined the Foreign Legion.

"Forget?" Sir Malcolm roared indignantly. "I
never forget anything! Damn it, my memory's better
than yours." He was raging at his son. He seemed to
have forgotten—or perhaps, not noticed—that I
was the one who had brought up the subject. "I've

never gone off and left a patient unattended in the chair, sirrah! Nor have I—"

"There you are, Malcolm." Sir Geoffrey entered briskly. "Could hear you five miles off with the wind blowing in the opposite direction. I knew you wouldn't forget me. Might have known"—he favoured Morgana Fane with a fine Edwardian leer—"you'd found something better to occupy your time than an old warhorse like me."

"Heh, heh, heh," Sir Malcolm said, suddenly becoming putty in his friend's competent hands. "Neat little filly, eh?"

"The best." Sir Geoffrey twirled his moustache. "Put my last shilling on her, any day."

Morgana blossomed, if I may use the expression. She wasn't sure who the newcomer was, but the aura of money and power was unmistakable. "You might introduce me, Malcolm," she said sweetly.

"See here." I drew Endicott Zayle to one side while these quaint Victorian rites were in progress. "We've got to have a conference. Don't say anything more until I can—"

"Eh? What?" Zayle stared at me with a glazed look. I couldn't really blame him. Sir Malcolm was enough to daze any beholder, even one who knew him so well as—presumably—his own son did.

"And who"—Morgana Fane was suddenly beside me again, looking up with a coquettishness obviously left over from the last introduction—"are you?"

When in doubt, stick to your story. "I'm an emergency," I said. "An emergency case, that is." A bright idea hit me, although I couldn't bring it off with Sir Geoffrey still there. But later, perhaps, when the timing had had a chance to fade and get confused, we might be able to plead that I was the reason Endicott Zayle had left his post. Another's need had been greater than Morgana's. I tucked the idea away for future reference.

"Good God, yes, lad!" Meanwhile, Sir Geoffrey backed me with vigour. "You were in a bad way. Has he seen to you yet?"

"Emergency?" Endicott Zayle's eyes brightened and began to focus properly for the first time that afternoon. "You? Yes, yes, of course." He gripped my arm firmly and began pulling me toward the chair. "Just come over here and let me look at you. We'll take care of it immediately."

"Hold it, hold it," I muttered to him, drawing back. "Don't get carried away. That was just the cover story—remember?"

"Cover story?" he said blankly. "What are you talking about? If you aren't an emergency, what are you doing here?"

"I've been asking myself the same question," I said, trying to hang on to what little equilibrium I had left. I didn't know what game Zayle was playing now, but it wasn't the one we'd started out with, and I was getting dizzier by the minute. It wouldn't take long before I was as dizzy as Zayle himself. I hoped it wouldn't affect me the same way—I had enough problems without imagining corpses.

"Oh, by the way." Reminded, I freed myself from Zayle's grip and turned to the healthiest corpse I'd ever seen. "I came up with a message for you, Miss Fane. Your business manager is getting anxious—something about being due at *Vogue*."

"Overdue is more like it." She glanced at her watch with a coo of dismay. "We're shooting a feature on my honeymoon. All the clothes I've chosen for my trousseau, out of all the fashion garments I've modeled recently."

I nodded admiringly. For the past several years she had been constantly in the company of the Title she was about to sweep in triumph to the Registrar's Office. And now she was going to cash in on honeymoon features. It was a masterpiece of the public relations art that any interest could be drummed up in such a fait accompli.

"Well, that *does* it," she said. "I can't waste time here any longer. *If*"—she gave Zayle a dismissive frown—"you find the time, you might make another appointment for me."

"Anytime at all, Miss Fane," he babbled. "I'm terribly sorry about this. Just come when you can— I'll fit you in. It's the least—"

I jabbed him sharply in the ribs and he had the sense to shut up.

We all watched her leave, but the others couldn't have appreciated her exit as much as I did. I was never so relieved in my life to see someone going out on their own two feet, instead of being carried out. Now all I had to worry about was ridding Zayle of this new idea that I needed instant and immediate dental treatment. If necessary, I was prepared to discourage it with a straight left to the jaw.

While the others were staring after Morgana Fane, still bemused, the intercom buzzed. Since no one else seemed inclined to answer it, I picked up the phone myself and listened to the receptionist's urgent question.

"No," I said. "Both Zayles are here, but Meredith isn't."

"He'll be in his own surgery," Endicott Zayle said. "The stupid girl has been here long enough to know that."

"She says he isn't," I told him. "She says she's been ringing and there's no answer. His next patient has just arrived, and he hasn't taken the previous one yet. She thought he might have been in conference with you."

More likely, she'd thought he must have been drawn in by the raised voices. They must have been audible downstairs, let alone in the next-door surgery. I began to feel a faint disquiet. Why hadn't Tyler Meredith come in to see what all the commotion was about? It was *his* new anaesthetic that was being tested, after all.

"His line may be out of order," Sir Geoffrey suggested. "Why not just pop in and sound the alert?"

En bloc, we moved toward the interconnecting door below the level of the small intersecting X-ray room. Endicott Zayle, I noticed, seemed unworried, but faintly distracted, as though recent events had been slightly beyond his grasp. Not that he was alone; it was all beyond my grasp, too.

It was the senior Zayle who took the doorknob with the same no-nonsense grip he might have used on a pair of forceps and swung the door open. "Wakey, wakey in there," he roared.

There was no response from the figure stretched

out in the dental chair. As we advanced farther into the room, we could see the mask—like an oxygen mask—strapped over his face; hear the hissing of the tank hooked into the wheeled stand. I didn't need to see the faint glitter of the partially open eyes to know that Tyler Meredith wasn't going to wake again.

"By God." General Sir Malcolm Zayle turned to his son and slapped him on the back. "You've done it, at last! I'm proud of you, m'boy!"

"Father, please!" Endicott Zayle seemed to shrivel. His head swiveled unbelievingly between the sight in the chair and the triumphant elder Zayle.

"Don't worry, Son, I'll stand by you! We'll get old Harry Stacey for the defence—very good on the Unwritten Law, old Harry." He turned to Sir Geoffrey for agreement. "Hasn't lost a case since Hector was a pup."

"Lord Stacey's dead, Malcolm," Sir Geoffrey said.

"What? Dead? What? Why wasn't I told?" Sir Malcolm demanded. "What happened, eh? Shot by a jealous husband, was that it?"

"Hardening of the arteries, Malcolm," Sir Geoffrey said sadly. "Life catches up with us all."

"Egad!" Sir Malcolm said. "I knew he was living too fast—but that! Why wasn't I told?" he demanded again.

"You were away, Father," Endicott said, a placating note I had never had occasion to hear before in his voice. "On active service. We sent word. Possibly, the post . . . "

"Damned post," Sir Malcolm said. "A man slogging his guts out on the field of honour, and not one letter in five ever reaching him with news of home. No wonder they say war is hell!"

"I'm sorry, Father," Endicott said. Beads of sweat were gathering along his receding hairline. "I—we—had no idea messages weren't reaching you."

I began to get a strange feeling in the pit of my stomach. Sir Malcolm was talking as though war were a contemporary event. For him. As though he were home on leave from some battlefield and expected to return to it at any moment. As for the others, I could see that Sir Malcolm was quite a formidable character, but need they humour him to this extent? I began to wonder whose hand actually controlled the purse strings at Zayle, Zayle & Meredith.

"Never mind." Sir Malcolm brushed trivialities aside. "We'll find the best man living to handle the defence. Then, I think, a spell in the service for you, m'boy. Enlist, that's the ticket. Everybody loves a soldier. Volunteer for the front line. Get wounded, if you can. A medal or two will put a lot of things right in civilian life."

"But, Father—" Endicott wailed. "It was suicide—it must have been."

"Be a man, m'boy," his father encouraged. "And don't worry—it will all be over by Christmas."

I'd stopped worrying about Sir Malcolm—he was Endicott's problem—and had started worrying about my own. I could understand how Tyler Meredith had come to commit suicide: if he'd glanced into the adjoining surgery to see how the experiment

with his new anaesthetic was going and found
Morgana Fane, to all intents and purposes, a corpse
in the chair, the failure of his formula and the resul-
tant publicity might have seemed too much to bear.

But how could I phrase a press release to that
effect in such a way that Morgana Fane didn't discover the worst about those paralysed moments she
had described so graphically in the dental chair? If
she were to realize that her own dentist had believed
her dead, had abandoned her after using her as a
guinea pig for a new anaesthetic, she would have
grounds for the biggest, most sensational lawsuit to
hit the Old Bailey in decades.

"Father—" Endicott Zayle bleated again. "Tyler
could only have committed suicide. Look at the way
he has the mask—it's strapped on. You know very
well that we're taught never to test a gas anaesthetic
by strapping on the mask. And never to sit in the
chair, either. We're supposed to stand on our feet and
hold the mask lightly to our faces. Then, if we're
overcome, we'll drop the mask as we fall. We'd never,
never—"

"Anaesthetics—never held with 'em!" Sir
Malcolm snarled. "Waste of time. Only reason they're
so popular today"—he turned to Sir Geoffrey—"is
because the younger generation is weak and flabby.
Can't pull a tooth the way *we* could. Have to have the
patient in a helpless position—unresisting."

"That's right, Malcolm," Sir Geoffrey agreed.
"I've noticed it myself. Personally, I wouldn't be too
hard on the young ones. I think it's due to a pro-
gressive muscular degeneration. You don't see a

right arm like yours these days. No village smithys, either."

"Too many horseless carriages, as well. They'll be losing the use of their legs next," Sir Malcolm said. They seemed to be settling down to a jolly little session about what was wrong with the younger generation, but before they convened the meeting, there was something they seemed to be losing sight of.

"Shouldn't we call the police?" I suggested.

"Who *is* this?" Sir Malcolm demanded. "What is he doing in my home at a time like this? Why isn't he in uniform?"

"It's all right, Malcolm," Sir Geoffrey said quickly. "He's my adjutant. His uniform hasn't come through yet. Shortages, you know."

"Damned government!" Sir Malcolm snorted. "Hell of a way to run a war!"

"The police—" I felt like someone in the trenches who had heard the "Charge" and was game, even though I knew someone had blundered.

"The police," I repeated, fixing Endicott with a glare that was intended to convey *better late than never.*

"The police," Endicott repeated weakly. "Do you think that's really necessary?"

"The fellow *is* dead," Sir Geoffrey said judiciously. There was no arguing with that diagnosis.

"Suddenly, and without a registered physician in attendance—if not under suspicious circumstances." I nudged Endicott severely. "There are laws about such things. The police will have to be notified."

"Quite right, quite right," Sir Malcolm said.

"Quite proper. The police are reasonable chaps. Don't worry, we'll get you off."

"Father," Endicott all but wailed, "stop saying that! I didn't do it. I didn't kill him."

"You didn't?" Sir Malcolm drew back, offended. "You're sure you didn't?"

"Father, I swear to you—" For one horrified moment, I thought Endicott was actually going to sink to his knees, but he contented himself with raising his right hand solemnly. "I swear to you I didn't do it!"

"Damn it all," Sir Malcolm said, "why not? The damned fella's been playing fast and loose with your wife for the past eighteen months!"

"Father!" Endicott reeled backward and I had to revise yet one more opinion. Sir Malcolm might not be sure exactly what decade he was in, but he was fully aware of what was happening in his immediate surroundings.

"Eh?" Something in Endicott's voice seemed to get through to Sir Malcolm. While Sir Geoffrey quietly went to the phone and dialed for an outside line, Sir Malcolm regarded his son with dissatisfaction. "You didn't?"

"I didn't," Endicott said firmly.

In the silence, I was conscious of the rhythmic clicking of the dial as the digits spun smoothly back to their places: *nine, nine, nine*.

I was also conscious of the body in the chair, long motionless beneath the deadly mask over its nose and mouth. Conscious, as well, of the back of that silent head. Of the noticeable lump at the base of the skull. It was what we laymen knew, in our nonmedical parlance, as a "goose egg." It suggested strongly that Tyler Meredith had been coshed before he had been lain in that chair and the mask strapped tightly over his face.

"You didn't," Sir Malcolm said. He seemed to be staring absently at the faintly purplish lump on Tyler Meredith's head. "Then," he asked, quite reasonably, "if you didn't, who did?"

Chapter 4

I got back to the office feeling like something the cat had dragged in.

The cat, however, sniffed and disowned me. Obviously still catching whiffs of antiseptic, she went to ground behind Gerry's ankles, muttering to herself.

I didn't really blame her. At the best of times, a dentist's surgery has never been redolent to me of fun and games. And this certainly hadn't been the best of times. After this afternoon, all I wanted was to get the clinging, lingering odours of antiseptic, anaesthetic, and death out of my nostrils.

Tugging my tie off, I headed straight for the bathroom and began running a bath. While it filled, I stripped off my clothes, dropping them in a heap on the floor.

Gerry followed me in. He began picking up my things and folding them neatly. I realized it was the measure of his concern—usually, he was the untidy one. I realized, too, that he had been talking to me since I came in. It wasn't that I'd been ignoring him, it was just that I'd had too much on my mind even to notice. I took a deep breath. Sooner or later, I was going to have to start explaining to him.

"That's it," Gerry said. "Get in the tub, lie back, soak for a while. Shall I get you a drink? Was it very bad? He didn't—he didn't *extract*, did he?"

It dawned on me that the whole episode had been so recent it wasn't even a "stop press" item yet. Gerry had found my rather ambiguous note and still assumed that I had visited the dentist for the usual legitimate reason.

I shook my head no to all his questions and kept on shaking it. Perhaps the exercise would clear it a bit.

Pandora stalked into the bathroom to find out why she was being neglected. She was appalled to find Gerry with an armload of clothes reeking of unpleasant associations. While I was now more socially acceptable, I was in the bath and out of reach, surrounded by water. In a fury, she sprang onto the low-suite cistern behind the toilet seat and perched there, reviling us both.

"You didn't hear the six-o'clock news?" I asked. "Or wasn't it mentioned? It might not have been. The first news will probably break in the morning editions." I tried to count my blessings. At least, Tyler Meredith's death wouldn't create the havoc of publicity Morgana Fane's would have.

"News?" Gerry twitched nervously. "You don't mean you made medical—er, dental—history, do you? My God! What went wrong?"

"It was murder," I said. "Sheer, bloody murder. There's no point in trying to deny it between ourselves."

"Hold on, old man," Gerry said. "Stay there—I'll be right back."

I heard the comforting clink of bottles from the other room. When he returned, Gerry was carrying two glasses of dark-amber fluid—not an easy task, as he was still absently clutching the clothes he had retrieved from the floor earlier. I stretched out an arm and relieved him of one of the glasses.

"Wrap yourself around that, old man," Gerry said sympathetically, "and then tell me. What did they do to you?"

"I'm all right," I said. "They never laid a drill on me." Not that Zayle hadn't tried hard enough—that was another nightmarish element to the endless afternoon. He'd evidently decided it would lend authenticity to our cover story if he got in some drillwork on me and had kept trying to jockey me into the chair—the unoccupied one. However, while I'm always willing to go along with an alibi—especially one I've invented myself—I draw the line at sacrificing a molar to it, and so he didn't succeed.

"Then what the hell's the matter with you?"

Gerry demanded. "You don't look as though you've been for a pleasant social interlude."

"I haven't," I said. "I told you—it was murder. But," I added hopefully, "I don't think the police realize that yet. And perhaps I'm wrong—that bruise on the back of his head *might* have been there for a couple of days. Anyway, we managed to get the General back upstairs and keep him there, so he couldn't spill the—"

Abruptly, Gerry reverted to type. Discovering he was still holding my clothes, he pulled up the lid of the laundry hamper and pitched them inside—suit and all. For good measure, he picked up my shoes and threw them in as well.

"Now," he said, "would you care to start at the beginning?"

"Zayle rushed in here this afternoon . . ." I lost the soap and stopped to look for it.

"Suppose," Gerry said with dangerous patience, "you get out of that bloody tub and come into the office where we can have a civilized conversation."

"No slippers," I said. I looked hopefully at Pandora. "I don't suppose your ladyship would oblige?"

Pandora gave me a haughty look and turned her head away. She was usually an agreeable little cat, but she steadfastly refused to fetch my slippers.

"For God's sake—you two!" Gerry stormed out of the room and returned with my robe and slippers, which he slammed down on the floor beside the tub. "Now, get out of it!"

I pulled the plug and reached for the towel.

Pandora padded after me as we went into the office, prepared to reclaim me as her own, now that I reeked decently of Castile soap and Scotch.

"Now"—Gerry seated himself behind the desk and faced me grimly—"let's have the worst."

"So," Gerry said as I finished, "dentists have begun murdering one another, have they? It couldn't happen to a better profession."

"Actually," I said, "I don't think Zayle *did* do it. I mean, he was *here* for quite a while. I'll swear he honestly believed he'd killed Morgana Fane with that new anaesthetic. If he wasn't convinced of it, then the stage lost a potential great when he chose dentistry. He certainly had *me* believing she was dead. It was one of the shocks of my life when she appeared in that doorway—"

"Please." Gerry shuddered. "Let's not borrow trouble. She's alive. You never heard—you never thought—you never dreamed—of anything else. The mere idea of trying to do a PR job to cover her demise in Zayle's chair is enough to send me to an earlier grave than Tyler Meredith's."

"Agreed," I said. "I mean, how could we possibly have explained . . . ?"

"*Prryow!*" Pandora chimed in. She leaped from my lap to my shoulder and settled there, purring comfortingly into my left ear.

"Let's forget that," Gerry said. "Let's just settle for what we *do* have to explain. Which is . . . ?" He paused delicately.

"I'm not sure yet," I admitted. "But it doesn't seem too bad—at the moment. In the circumstances, there'll have to be autopsy, I suppose. But even if the pathologist does come to the worst conclusion, we ought to be pretty well out of it. I mean, it may be an item, but it's scarcely headline material. A dentist dies, under slightly shady conditions—who's going to be passionately interested?"

"Exactly," Gerry concurred. "It may be unfortunate, but it's scarcely earthshaking. Let's have another drink."

We were just relaxing nicely when the doorbell rang. We looked at each other and tossed a mental coin. As usual, I lost. Pandora registered a strong protest as I rose and crossed to open the door. I should have listened to her.

Endicott Zayle stood there. For a wild moment, I considered slamming the door in his face and pretending there was no one at home, but something told me that idea wasn't feasible.

"Er . . . come in," I said feebly.

"Thank you." He sidled inside with suspicious obsequity.

Pandora shifted on my shoulder and began to inch backward, growling faintly, until she had put my neck between her and the intruder. He might be almost unrecognizable in a suit instead of his white jacket, and no antiseptic could compete with the waves of shaving lotion he had splashed on, but she knew that there was something about that man she didn't like.

I was with her one hundred percent. *We do not like thee, Dr. Zayle.* I tried to force my face into an expression that was noncommittal, if not exactly welcoming.

"Yes?" I said. I couldn't quite manage "Good evening."

"I was just passing by," he said unconvincingly, "and I thought I'd drop in and see how you were. We weren't able to get to that tooth of yours this afternoon because of all the confusion. How is it? Still holding up, eh?"

I might have thought a gentle madness was setting in—if I couldn't see the expression on Gerry's face. No, I was all right, and things hadn't changed since the last time I'd noticed. Dentists *didn't* make house calls. Which left the madness on the other foot.

"It's fine." I tried to recall Zayle to sanity. "It always was fine. Don't you remember? We just agreed to—"

"Ah-ha-ha-ha, silly of me." His eyes were fixed on a spot just below my left ear. I realized Pandora was peeking around my neck at him, still snarling softly. "Of course . . . of course." He kept staring at Pandora as though he'd never seen her before. Perhaps he hadn't; she'd spent all of his last visit under the desk.

Then I clearly recalled his stooping to see what the hissing was and remaining crouched, staring into her eyes. Perhaps he just had a thing about Siamese cats.

"Actually . . . ," he said, and I braced myself for the crunch. "Actually . . . I'm meeting Adele—my wife—at Charing Cross Station in half an hour. Since you were just across the street, I thought . . . "

"You thought you'd drop in for a drink while you

were waiting." Gerry went to get another glass. "Very sensible of you, old man."

"My wife—Adele," Zayle continued babbling, "has been visiting friends on the coast. She'll be expecting to be met. She'll be expecting . . . " He trailed off limply.

She'll be expecting Tyler Meredith, my mind finished the sentence automatically. There were also a few likely follow-up sentences lingering around my brain, but I tried to ignore them.

"Here you are, old man." Gerry thrust the drink at him, but his voice had lost some of its heartiness. He, too, had begun to suspect what was coming next.

"Thank you. Cheers." Zayle didn't look as though he'd ever see cheer in anything again.

"I thought—" he said. "That is, I was wondering—I mean, it's only across the street—"

While Zayle was floundering, I met Gerry's eyes and he shrugged resignedly. It was plain to see that either we were all going to meet Adele's train together, or we'd have Endicott Zayle around our necks all night. He wasn't going to have enough courage to face his wife alone. Far less, break the bad news all by himself. And as he had said, it was only across the street. There were disadvantages in living near a Main Line station, too.

"If you could just meet the train with me," he pleaded. "It wouldn't take long. Just—just stand by for a few minutes. I—I'll have to tell her before she gets back to the house. Er . . . you might like," he added hopefully, "to drive back with us. I—I could return your hospitality then."

"Sorry, that's out," Gerry said firmly. "Pressure of work. The station, yes. Anything else, no."

"Yes, quite." Zayle accepted the ultimatum with a sigh. He would be on his own with his Adele once the train disembarkation was over. He did not appear to be enjoying the prospect.

"Excuse me." I bent and sloped my shoulders, decanting a protesting Pandora onto the desktop. "I'll go and get dressed."

We saved a lot of time and effort by using the side entrance, the long flight of steps leading up from Villiers Street into Charing Cross Station itself. Only a couple of trains were in. The station was quiet, recovering from the rush-hour exodus.

"Platform tickets," Zayle muttered. "We must have platform tickets." He fussed over to a machine and busied himself with a handful of change. Gerry and I stood where he had left us, waiting until, in his own good time—which seemed longer than necessary—he came back to us.

"Here you are. And you. And one for me." He doled out the platform tickets like a Nanny. I almost expected to hear "What do you say?" when neither of us bothered with a thank-you.

But his mind was on other things. "Platform five." He looked around vaguely. "Platform five—the train should be arriving soon."

As though to underline his words, the loudspeaker announced the train arriving at Platform 5.

"Over there." We sprinted down the platform, waving our platform tickets as we passed the ticket gate, then halted as the train slowed to a stop.

Carriage doors began to slam along the length of the train, and Zayle backed up suddenly, stopping as he collided with us.

"Sorry," he said nervously. "Sorry." Despite the fact that he had us with him for moral support, he looked as though he'd like to cut and run. He glanced up and down the platform in increasing agitation. "Do you see her?" he asked.

"We don't know what she looks like," I reminded him. "We've never met your wife." Our visits to him had always been businesslike, brief and to the point. We had never felt like lingering, after the drill had been removed and the mouth rinsed, for any social chitchat.

"Oh?" He seemed vaguely surprised. "Haven't you?" He looked down the platform again and tried to take another step backward, but I was in his way. "Here she comes now," he said.

With us flanking him, he moved forward to intercept a statuesque redhead who was hurrying toward the ticket gate. She was looking over and beyond us, craning her neck to see a face she was expecting. It was obviously a shock, and not a pleasant one, when Zayle stepped into her path.

"Hello, dear," he said. "Did you have a nice holiday?" He reached for her suitcase.

"Oh!" She stopped short and for a moment we all stood there, making an immovable little island, being buffeted around the edges by the departing passengers.

"Shall we step out of the way?" Zayle suggested, trying to give her time to recover. Silently, we moved to the far side of the platform, beside the empty bay, which would not be empty for long. Even now, the loudspeaker was announcing the imminent arrival of a train at Platform 6.

"Where's Tyler?" Adele asked abruptly. "Why isn't he here? What have you done with him?" She turned a cool, level look on me and then on Gerry, still flanking Zayle, but didn't bother to ask who we were or what we were doing there. We were of no interest to her.

"Darling, I'd like you to meet Doug and Gerry," Zayle babbled desperately. "They're my—" He broke off, evidently realizing that he could not admit that he felt the need of a couple of public relations men in order to greet his own wife. "Uh—I've known them a long time," he finished limply.

"I see." We were still of no interest to her. She lifted her eyes thoughtfully to the distant horizon of intersecting steel rails. At the far end of the platform bay, a train slowed and curved into the bay, heading for home base.

"Did you have a good journey? Would you like a drink before we start home? How are—"

"It's no use, Endicott," she said. "I've come to a decision."

"Please, Adele." He frowned warningly. "Not here. Can't it wait until we get home?"

"Since you forced the issue by appearing here like this," she said, "it can't. I'm sorry"—she tossed a perfunctory apology to Gerry and me—"but he brought you along because he thought I wouldn't make a scene in front of strangers. He's just using you. He's like that, you know."

We nodded glumly. We knew.

"Now, really, Adele—"

"No, Endicott," she said firmly. "You might as well know now. I want a divorce. I'm going to marry Tyler just as soon as it can be arranged."

"Oh, no!" Zayle gave the impression of reeling. "No—you can't."

I felt a bit like reeling myself. This was going to be worse than I had expected—and I had expected the worst.

"Oh, yes, I can, Endicott. And I wouldn't advise you to try to stop me. There's absolutely nothing you can do. My decision is final."

"No." Zayle looked helplessly from Gerry to me. "No . . . it's impossible."

I saw, with a cold and deadly clarity, just why Zayle had stopped by for us. He had no intention of breaking the news to her himself. He was waiting for one of us to do it. I looked at Gerry. I'd done my fair whack for the day—let him start earning his own chunks of silver amalgam.

"*Nothing* is impossible," Adele Zayle said coldly. "Least of all this."

"Actually, Mrs. Zayle," Gerry said, "I'm afraid it is. I'm sorry, but there's been an accident. Mr. Meredith—"

"He's dead, Adele." Zayle could not conceal his triumph. "Tyler's dead."

"Nonsense!" But she went white and cold as marble. "That can't be true. I was talking to him just after lunch. He answered the telephone himself. He was perfectly all right then."

"It happened sometime this afternoon," I said.

"No one can be quite sure when. After the autopsy, the police might—"

"Autopsy? Police?" She glared from one to another of us. " That doesn't sound like an accident. It was—murder?"

I kept silent. After what I had seen, I didn't want to answer that question. I waited for Zayle to deny it, hoping he could sound convincing. I'd like to be convinced myself.

He didn't say anything. He just kept staring at his wife with that odd expression in which there was more than a trace of satisfaction and triumph.

"You did it!" she accused. "If Tyler's dead, then you killed him. Why are you here? Why haven't the police arrested you? Unless—?" She looked hopefully at Gerry and me.

"No," I denied quickly. We might look fairly official, flanking Zayle as we were, but I hoped we didn't look as though we had him in custody. "No, we're public relations consultants."

"You needn't look so smug," Adele flared at her husband. "You're not going to get away with it."

Before either of us could guess what she was going to do, she stepped forward, put both hands against Zayle's chest and shoved. Then, without looking back, she snatched up her suitcase and walked off.

We caught him just in time. Off balance, he teetered over the track in front of the oncoming train, while we each pulled desperately at an arm. One concerted heave, and we had him back on the safety of the platform while the train slid past.

"Oh, dear," he said, looking after his departing wife. "I was afraid she'd be upset."

Neither he nor she looked behind at the platform bay, where steel wheels ground against steel rails over the spot where his body would have been lying if we hadn't been quick enough.

"Let that be a lesson to you, old boy." Over Zayle's head, Gerry said to me warningly, "Always beware of redheads—especially smoldering redheads."

Chapter 5

Our brush with a hot-tempered redhead seemed to have put Gerry in a thoughtful frame of mind where what's laughingly known as "the weaker sex" were concerned. At any rate, he actually spent the evening in the flat and was on tap at roll call in the morning. Consequently, we got a fair amount of work accomplished before little Penny, our secretary, arrived just after lunch, having spent her morning in secretarial school.

I was on the telephone, assuring an eager journalist that I would definitely let him know if the rumour about one of our clients turned out to be true. While miming to Penny that yes-I-was-all-right and no-the-dentist-hadn't-hurt-very-much, I made a mental note to check with said client and discover, if possible, what the hell was actually going on.

Before I disentangled myself, Penny was sitting down typing out a couple of press releases for Gerry. Foolishly thinking the coast was clear, I wandered over to the files to check the last known address of the peripatetic client in question.

That was when Penny answered the phone and betrayed that I was in.

"Yes," I heard her say, "he's right here." She extended the receiver to me with her most sympathetic look. "Mr. Zayle for you," she murmured.

I took the phone; it was too late to do anything else. I should have cut off the reporter and clued her in as soon as she appeared. What did alienating one of the major dailies matter, compared to being trapped like this?

"Perkins here," I admitted.

"You've got to *do* something," the frantic voice greeted me, without wasting time on pleasantries. "The police are coming back, Father's in one of his moods again, Adele has locked herself in her room, I've had reporters on the phone, and my nurse is still out sick. *Do something.*"

I took a deep breath.

"Are you there? Can you hear me? I said—"

"Yes, yes, I know," I said. "I heard you."

"Well, what are you going to *do*?" he demanded.

I took another deep breath and, discarding the

first few answers that rose to the tip of my tongue, tried for a balanced, soothing tone. "We"—I wasn't going to go into this alone—"we'll be over as soon as we can make arrangements about the office. Will that suit you?"

"I suppose it will have to," he said petulantly. "But be quick about it, can't you? What am I supposed to do, here by myself, carrying a double work load, without even a nurse—"

"As soon as we can." I eased the receiver back into the cradle and met Penny's bright, expectant gaze. It gave me an idea about the easiest-solved of Zayle's problems.

"What are your feelings," I asked her, "about dentists?"

"*Ee-yick!*" she replied, like any right-minded individual.

"I don't mean going to them," I corrected. "I mean working for them—being subleased, as it were. For a nice little bonus, of course," I added hastily. Gerry and I might be forfeiting our quids for the pro quos, but Penny wasn't included in the arrangement. We ought to be able to bill for her time—if she was willing.

"Oh, I don't mind *that*," she agreed cheerfully. "It's only the other end of the drill I object to."

"Right," I said, reaching for my all-too-thin notecase. "Grab a taxi and get over to Zayle, Zayle and Meredith. Tell Zayle you'll stand in for his nurse, and Gerry and I will be along as soon as we clear up a couple of odds and ends."

●　　●　　●

The waiting room was crowded by the time we arrived in midafternoon. Some of yesterday's contingent appeared to be there, with a smattering of new faces. Morgana Fane was absent—and who could blame her? After yesterday's experience, she had my complete sympathy if she elected to go through the rest of her life toothless. It was only fortunate that she hadn't realized how close to the Pearly Gates those pearly teeth had brought her.

While the receptionist was grappling uncertainly with basic facts ("Endicott Zayle is expecting us—No, we're not patients—He'll want us to go straight up—It's quite in order"), Penny strode into the waiting room, looking brisk and medical in a starched white coverall.

"Next," she announced crisply. The word was enough to make me shudder. Our Penny seemed to have donned a bloodless professionalism with the starched uniform. It made her less Our Penny.

"Oh, Mr. Perkins." She discovered me as she would have discovered a stranger loitering too near the silver. "Mr. Zayle says you're to wait in his private sitting room with Mr. Tate. Upstairs." She flicked her eyes heavenward momentarily, then narrowed them on the next victim.

"Oh, Mr. Johnson." She swooped on a reluctant patient, sniffing suspiciously. "You're to come right up. Mr. Zayle says he hopes you haven't been naughty and stopped for a drink before you came— you *know* you're a bleeder."

Gerry and I exchanged chastened glances and followed Penny and her victim up the narrow stairs.

"At the top of the next flight," she called back encouragingly to us, shepherding the unfortunate Mr. Johnson ahead of her. "Mr. Zayle will be along as soon as he can.

"No, not you, Mr. Johnson." She caught her reluctant patient by the arm as he swerved to try to follow us up the second flight of stairs. "Mr. Zayle is waiting for *you* right in here."

Looking back, I could see that she was ushering the patient into Tyler Meredith's surgery. It gave me a start for a moment, then I realized that, of course, Zayle was having to double up on the work with his partner dead and no time to arrange for a locum. It was understandable that he would be using both surgeries. He had sometimes done it in the past, when his partner was taking a holiday. Many's the time I'd been given an injection and left until it took effect, while Zayle darted into the next office to work on another patient whose injection had been given earlier and whose jaw had reached the required state of numbness.

The lounge on the next floor was unexpectedly cozy, with a blazing fire and a tea trolley waiting beside it. I wondered if Adele had come out of her sulk enough to decide to play hostess. The room was empty, though. We went in and sat down.

"Do you suppose we're intended to help ourselves?" Gerry was eyeing a plate of sandwiches and another of cakes nearly as greedily as I was. Lunch had been on the skimpy side.

I hoped Adele wouldn't be long if she was coming. I leaned forward and tested the heat of the teapot with my hand. It was very hot, which augured well for the imminent return of the hostess.

"Let's wait a bit," I said. "This must just have been brought in. Someone will probably be along in a minute."

A door at the far side of the room opened immediately. Expecting Adele, I rose to my feet. Gerry had been sitting farther back than I, and when he saw it was only a man, he gave up the struggle to rise. Men, even of advanced age, didn't rate the same courtesies as birds in Gerry's books.

"Ah!" Sir Malcolm strode into the room and snapped me a salute. Out of sheer surprise, I returned it. "At ease, lad." He sat down, and I took this to mean that I could sit down, too, although I was slightly out-of-date on military protocol. On second thought, I had never been current with the protocol General Sir Malcolm was operating under. I suspected the army had undergone considerable changes in the past forty years.

"Tea, eh? Excellent! Excellent!" He rubbed his hands together in brisk anticipation. "What kind of sandwiches have we?"

"They seem to be"—I checked—"pâté, egg salad, chicken, and ham."

"Aaah, wonderful housekeeper, that gal. Marvelous how she manages through the shortages. Smartest thing Endicott ever did when he married her. A looker, too."

"That's true," Gerry agreed, always glad to weigh in with a connoisseur's opinion, although I could see that part of the statement had him vaguely puzzled.

"What's that?" After one venomous glance upon entering, Sir Malcolm had ignored Gerry. Now he concentrated his attention upon him. He didn't appear to like what he saw.

"I said that's true," Gerry repeated. "The lady is a looker. She's got a nasty temper, though."

"Temper? Pah! Spirit!" Sir Malcolm glared at him. "More than you can claim, eh? What's a healthy young man like you doing here? Why aren't you Up Front?"

"Up Front?" Gerry was completely lost. I'd had so much to fill him in on last night, I hadn't got round to the details on Sir Malcolm's hazy grasp of the time of the century. He only knew that the old boy had a couple of idiosyncrasies that would constitute him an unreliable witness. "Is that a new boutique?"

Fortunately, Penny came in just then. "Mr. Zayle sent me up to pour," she announced, not knowing what a welcome diversion she was creating. We turned to her with relief.

Except Sir Malcolm, although he frowned less sternly at her. "Where's Nurse?" he demanded.

"She's joined up," Penny said. "I'm too young to go, so I'm taking her place on the home front to relieve her for duty." She raised her eyes to some red-white-and-blue horizon, sucked in her cheeks, and posed there looking impossibly soulfully noble. I could see that she was fully in the picture.

"Good girl!" Sir Malcolm beamed on her. "With

spirit like that in our youth, how can we lose?" he demanded of me.

"We didn't," I said. Penny's cheeks quivered. Gerry sat there, slowly shaking his head from side to side, as though to clear it—I knew the feeling.

"Are you going to start pouring?" I asked Penny.

"All right." She reverted to her normal cheerfulness and picked up the teapot.

"Three lumps, m'dear," Sir Malcolm said. "That is, if the ration's up to it."

"There's plenty," Penny said, sugaring it and handing him his cup. "*He*"—she gestured toward me with the teapot before serenely pouring—"doesn't take sugar." She passed me my sugarless tea with a smile which wasn't quite sweet enough to substitute.

"Excellent," Sir Malcolm said. "Excellent. We all have to make sacrifices in times like these, eh?"

"*I*," Gerry said firmly, surfacing enough to realize a fast shuffle was going on, "take three." As he leaned forward to take the cup, his ruffled cuff, linked with the gilt filigree and diamanté links some hopeful bird had given him, shot out from his sleeve. It was too late to signal to him. I leaned back, closed my eyes, and waited for the explosion. It came almost immediately.

"Young man," Sir Malcolm thundered, "are those ruffles? And is that"—he leaned forward for a closer, incredulous look—"a *flowered* shirt?"

"As a matter of fact, yes," Gerry said brightly. "Yes, to both questions. Seersucker printed with sprigs of forget-me-nots on pale lemon. They had primrose on lilac, but I thought this was subtler." He was beaming happily, ready to swap sartorial chatter, feeling that he had got onto the old boy's wavelength at last.

"Disgraceful!" Sir Malcolm snarled. "A young man like you—why aren't you in uniform?"

"I thought I was," Gerry said. "We can't all be in the pinstripe-and-bowler brigade, you know."

"What brigade?" General Sir Malcolm snapped to attention, eyes narrowing in suspicion. "I don't know them. Are they part of the regular army?"

"No, just regular civilians," Gerry said. He looked from me to Penny and back again. "What *is* this, anyway?"

"Ah, tea!" Endicott Zayle entered, rubbing his hands together in unconscious imitation of his father. "Just what I need right now. Very strong, no sugar, please."

"What about your patients?" I asked.

"Oh, they won't want any," he chuckled. "Neither of them could close their lips over the rim of a cup at this moment—Oh, oh, I see what you mean. No, they're all right. Just relaxing while the procaine takes effect. They'll never miss me for a few minutes. Each one will think I'm with the other." He gnawed into a chicken sandwich with zest, accepting the cup of tea Penny had poured for him.

"By the way," he said to her. "You might take a tray along to my wife, if you would. Just leave it outside her door, knock, and go away." It sounded as though it were a regular routine. "She'll take it in when she's ready."

"Locked her in her room again, have you?" Sir

Malcolm stopped brooding over Gerry, transferring his attention to his son. "Best place for her. Stop her from running after that other fella. And in your own house, too. I always said your Cynthia needed a strong hand—stronger than you have."

"Father," Endicott Zayle said, in some anguish, "Cynthia was my mother."

"No need to talk like that, m'boy." Sir Malcolm stiffened in offence. "She *is* your wife, you know. I thought she was a bit long in the tooth when you married her, but you made her Mrs. Zayle. Bite the bullet, m'boy, and live with it, but we won't have that sort of remark around here. Gentlemen don't speak about ladies in that manner, especially their wives."

"*Adele* is my wife," Zayle said feebly, as though conscious he was fighting the rearguard action to a losing battle.

"Flighty little piece." Sir Malcolm slipped smoothly from one reputation to another. "Always running after that fella. Mistake to have him in the house—I always said so."

Wisely, Penny disappeared with a tray. It would be nice if I could do the same, but duty forbade. "Have the police come back yet?" I asked.

"Police?" Sir Malcolm whirled to face me. "What police?"

"You remember, Father," Endicott said wearily. "They were here yesterday."

"About that blackout curtain again, eh? I warned you it wasn't secure enough. Have the whole damned blitzkrieg around our necks, if you aren't careful."

I noted with interest that he had slipped from

one war to another, mixing them as easily as he had mixed the ladies in his past. He was, perhaps, even more confused than I had bargained for. It was pointless then to read up on World War I, as I had intended doing if we were to spend much time in the Zayle ménage. Obviously, the only thing to do was to try to follow General Sir Malcolm Zayle—at a respectful distance—through whichever time belt he was straying at any given moment. A skimming knowledge of history, plus a generous dollop of child psychology, might be all that was necessary. The main thing was to swim with the tide, rather than try to struggle against it, as Endicott Zayle was doing right now.

"Father," he said urgently, "you *must* remember—it was only yesterday—"

Sir Malcolm looked at him coldly. "I have an excellent memory," he stated.

I agreed with him there. It was one of the best memories I had ever encountered, although a bit too selective for practicality. I was glad it was Endicott's problem, and not mine.

"They came about Tyler, Father."

"Tyler? Tyler—who?"

Endicott groaned, and I couldn't blame him. He inhaled deeply and seemed about to pursue the subject further when the door opened.

"Look who's here!" Penny popped her head inside, announcing the newcomer with more enthusiasm than formality. She skipped to one side, with a flourish of her hand, like the conjurer's assistant in a magic act.

I could have done without the cute little trick she had conjured up. Our old acquaintance, the ailurophobe policeman, walked through the doorway and stopped short at seeing Gerry and me. It was obvious that the sight of us had given him pause—and a very nasty pause, at that.

After a second, he moved forward again. "I thought she looked familiar," he said, "but a young girl like that might have changed her job." *She*, his tone implied, was young enough to reform.

"Hello," I said. It was very original, but I doubted that he would appreciate sterling wit. Not from me, certainly—and he didn't look enthusiastic about anyone else in the room, either.

He walked over to me, frowned, and reaching out, removed a couple of short shining hairs from my shoulder. "Still got that cat, I see," he observed.

"I'll give her your love," I said.

He grunted and turned away. This brought him face-to-face with Gerry, which he evidently didn't consider any improvement. He nodded and turned again. This time he was in front of Sir Malcolm; he seemed to feel he could face him. Unfortunately, it wasn't mutual.

"Young man." Sir Malcolm rose, giving the impression of towering over him. "Why aren't you in uniform?"

"I'm plainclothes—C.I.D. If you'd like to see my warrant card—"

"Young slackers!" Sir Malcolm looked to his son. "Why must we have these people in the house? They're a disgrace to King and Country!"

"Please, Father." Endicott Zayle started forward. "Why don't you go up to your quarters? This has nothing to do with you—"

"It has everything to do with me, if you're encouraging slackers and—"

Endicott had his father by one arm. I closed in and took the other arm. Together, we managed to extract him from the room without actually using force and get him upstairs to the austere bachelor quarters he occupied at the top of the house.

Chapter 6

When we returned to the sitting room, we found that the gentleman from the C.I.D. had made a start on his case by questioning Gerry. Since Gerry hadn't been present yesterday, this hadn't improved the shining hour very much, and both were in a rather disgruntled state.

"*You* were here at the time," he greeted me accusingly.

"Not at the time, no," I disclaimed heartily. "I arrived afterwards. He was dead when we found him."

"Do you know when he died?"

"No."

"Then how do you know you arrived afterwards?"

It was a question I would rather not think about. In fact, I knew from past experience, he wasn't going to ask me many questions I would be happy to think about. It was unfortunate that our past experience wasn't farther back in the past. He obviously hadn't had time to take a philosophical view of it.

"You don't need me right now, do you?" Endicott Zayle asked. "I have patients waiting." He backed hopefully toward the door, without waiting for a reply.

"I'll want to see you later. As soon as my sergeant gets the car parked, we'll want to go over a few points from yesterday."

"Yesterday . . . ?" Endicott Zayle said weakly, giving the impression that yesterday was more remote to him than the distant world his father lived in. I couldn't blame him. I'd be just as glad to forget yesterday myself.

"Meanwhile, I believe you said your wife was returning from a holiday last night. I'd like to speak to her now, if I might. That is," he added, as Endicott looked stricken, "if she's here."

"Oh, oh, yes, she's here. But I don't know—I mean, she's not feeling very well—I don't think—" Considering that his wife was the guilty party, Endicott was putting on a performance that would have made lesser mortals than a policeman immediately suspicious. "She's unavailable," he ended up, with sudden firmness.

"Perhaps, if we wait awhile, she'll become available. We have plenty of time." *Time enough to dig up the cellar, if necessary,* his tone implied. For a detective, he ran as nasty a line in innuendos as an undertipped headwaiter.

"Oh. Yes. No. Yes." Endicott jittered, catching some of the drift. "I'll call her." He glanced toward the door and his nerve faltered. "You call her," he said to me.

I wasn't any too pleased at the thought of encountering that redheaded temper again myself. Everyone was looking at me, however—Gerry with more sympathy than the others—and I decided to get out of sight before the inspector remembered he had been asking me questions when he got sidetracked. I'd do practically anything to keep him sidetracked, and fetching Adele ought to take care of it.

The tea tray, which had been standing outside the door, was gone. Taken inside while the coast was clear, I presumed.

"Mrs. Zayle." I tapped lightly on the door. "Mrs. Zayle?"

I hadn't really expected anything but silence on the first few attempts. After about five minutes of steady effort, she responded.

"Go away!"

I would have loved to. "Mrs. Zayle," I said. "The police are here."

"Police?"

"About Tyler Meredith," I said. "They want to speak to you."

The door opened abruptly. "And *I* want to speak to *them*!" She swept past me. I noted that, although she was dressed in black, she had taken enough time at some point in the day to apply full makeup.

I followed her, arriving in the doorway just behind her. I saw that the sergeant was there now, having evidently parked the car successfully, but that Endicott Zayle hadn't yet succeeded in getting away to his waiting patients.

"Dear, are you . . . feeling better?" Zayle inquired tentatively. "This is Detective Chief Inspector Rennolds. He'd like to talk to you for a minute, ask you a few questions. I told him you weren't really up to it, but he insisted. Inspector, my wife, Adele."

"How do you do?" she said perfunctorily. "Arrest that man!"

Not surprisingly, the inspector goggled. She was pointing at her husband.

"I was afraid she was still upset," Endicott said, to no one in particular.

"Why?" Inspector Rennolds asked, showing that practical streak of his again.

"Because he killed Tyler Meredith."

"Did you see him do it?" It occurred to me that the inspector had encountered redheads before.

"No, of course not. I've been out of town."

"Did he confess to you that he'd done it?"

"No!" she stamped her foot impatiently. "Why are you wasting time with all these silly questions? Why don't you arrest him? He had everything— motive, means, and opportunity. What more do you want?"

"Juries like proof," the inspector said. He glanced at Endicott Zayle with some sympathy. "You can go back to your patients now. They'll be wondering what's happened to you."

"Yes, but Adele—"

"She'll be all right. We're just going to have a little discussion." He looked over at Gerry and me. "You can go, too, but don't go far. I'll want to talk to you again later."

"We'll be downstairs in the waiting room," I said. As we left the room, I heard Adele begin to explain that she and Tyler Meredith were engaged, that she had intended to divorce her husband and marry Tyler. I caught the slightly glazed expression on Inspector Rennolds's face just before the door closed behind us. He looked like a man who had heard it all before.

Everyone in the waiting room looked up as we entered, then looked away again, dissatisfied. Some of them had been waiting an inordinately long time. Even the appearance of the receptionist to say "You're next" would have been welcome.

"You were here yesterday!" Until the Hon. Edytha Cale-Cunningham spoke to me suddenly, I hadn't recognized her. Now I was shocked. Yesterday she had just appeared nervous and highly strung; today she was haggard and hagridden. There were dark shadows under her eyes, and a protective layer of flesh had disappeared between bones and skin, leaving her gaunt.

"Have you heard what happened?" She came over to me, clutching my arm urgently with a hand that was little more than a claw. "Do you *know*?"

I didn't feel like admitting how much I did

know—especially to her. "I've . . . er . . . heard that Endicott Zayle . . . lost his . . . partner," I evaded.

"I shall never believe it was suicide!" The claw tightened on my arm. "Never!"

I met Gerry's look and we tacitly agreed that we wanted to get the hell out of here. The question was how to pry myself loose before those tourniquet fingers cut off my circulation.

"You don't believe it"—the shadowed eyes gazed up at me beseechingly—"do you?"

"I hardly knew the man," I said quickly. "I was always one of Zayle's patients." It had been a great mistake to come down here. We should have gone upstairs and joined Sir Malcolm—at least I had learned how to cope with him adequately. A couple of hours lurching down Memory Lane after him would have been child's play compared to this.

"*I* knew him," she said. "That's why I know he would never have committed suicide. I knew him very well. We"—her voice lowered confidentially— "we were engaged. We were going to be married."

That threw me. "Congratulations," I said, then realized that wasn't the right thing to say. "I mean— I'm sorry," I said hastily, but that didn't sound right, either. I looked to Gerry for help.

He was carefully looking in another direction. Which meant it had thrown him, too.

"So, you see," the Honourable Edytha continued, "*I* knew him better than anyone. Especially"—her tone hardened—"better than Mr. Zayle, who's been spreading this terrible rumour. There was a tremendous amount of jealousy there, you know. Professional jealousy. Tyler was so much better at his work than Mr. Zayle."

I decided to let that pass. If Tyler Meredith had convinced her that Zayle's jealousy was for professional reasons only, it wasn't up to me to make any enlightening remarks. I had a feeling, though, that Inspector Rennolds was going to have some very interesting moments in the not-too-distant future.

"The police are upstairs," I said. "Investigating further." She was entitled to know that much; she would have discovered it soon, in any case. "I think you ought to talk to them. They'll want to know what you've just been telling me."

"Police?" She looked startled, almost frightened. As though she had not followed her thought through to its logical conclusion. Perhaps she had persuaded herself that Meredith's death had been an accident. It had been intended to look like one.

"Police . . ." She drew a shaky breath. "Yes, yes, I suppose I must. It's my duty to tell them everything."

"It's always the best course to take," I said. "Telling the police everything, I mean." I thought of all I hadn't told them and restrained a wince. They still believed my presence here yesterday was due to a sudden toothache. For as long as possible, I intended to allow them to go on believing that. I couldn't see that dragging Morgana Fane into the already complex proceedings would do anything but confuse the issue. Not to mention giving her grounds for a possible malpractice suit. Poor Zayle had enough problems without that.

"Before I do," she said earnestly, "there's something I'd like to attend to first." She relaxed her grip on my arm and I felt the blood begin to flow again. I made a mental bet that I'd have bruises when I looked.

"I'm sure that will be all right," I agreed recklessly. It wasn't up to me to chase Inspector Rennolds's informants up to him.

"Thank you," she said. She seemed to feel that I had given her some sort of official permission. "I just want to go up to Tyler's flat. There are several things—keepsakes—I'd like to have. Also, a few belongings of my own I want to retrieve. Nothing that could possibly be of importance to anyone else." The muscles of her face twitched, curling the corners of her mouth upward in a bright, unconvincing smile. She nodded graciously to me and still nodding, walked out into the hallway and started upstairs.

We watched her go. The others in the waiting room paid no attention. There was no reason why they should. Our conversation had been carried on in a fairly discreet undertone.

"You know," Gerry said thoughtfully, "I'm not so sure we should have let her go. Alone, that is. Suppose she removes a lot of stuff the police need for evidence. They won't like that."

"And we're not very popular with them as it is." I saw his point. Although the Honourable Edytha probably only wanted to retrieve nothing more incriminating than a few wisps of chiffon, the police would undoubtedly prefer everything to remain where it was until they had had a chance to go over the flat.

"Perhaps," I suggested hopefully, "they'll have sealed the flat so that no one can get in."

"I doubt it," Gerry said. "It wasn't the scene of the crime. In fact," he added, "they haven't even sealed *that* off. Zayle has been using it all day."

"You think we ought to do something about it?"

"Either stop her, or go and tell Rennolds what she's doing and let him take over."

I considered the choices briefly. "I'd rather try to stop her." She was less formidable.

"Right." We left the waiting room and started up the stairs. There was no one in sight. I wondered vaguely where the receptionist had disappeared to, but thought she might have stepped out for a minute. It might even be her turn to be questioned by Inspector Rennolds.

The coast was clear as we skimmed past the second-floor living quarters. The third floor hallway was also deserted; all the doors leading off it were tightly shut. We looked at each other and shrugged.

"Might as well have a go," Gerry said. "Knock and don't wait for an answer—that's the ticket." He stepped up to the door of what, judging from the rooms below, must be the living room and knocked firmly. Equally firmly, he grasped the doorknob and turned it before the knock had finished echoing.

Nothing happened.

"Damn!" Gerry tried again. "Locked."

I moved across the hall and tried another door. It didn't yield. By this time, I'd decided it was hopeless, but just in case, I tried the remaining doors.

"It's no use," I said. "They're all locked. She's in

there, either having a quiet weep or destroying evidence. Either way, she doesn't want company."

"She may be doing both," Gerry said brightly. "Never underestimate the ability of the female mind to travel along several tracks at the same time. It may be why some of them are such terrifying drivers."

"Of course"—I had another thought—"the place may have been locked up before she got here. She might not have been able to get in."

"Highly unlikely." Gerry looked at me thoughtfully. "That just proves how old-fashioned you are. These days, a bird gets the latchkey long before the subject of a ring comes up. You don't appreciate how forbearing I've had to be with my birds in order to spare your privacy. Some of them haven't taken it at all well."

"I wouldn't call the Honourable Edytha a bird." I attacked the portion of his statement I considered most relevant at this moment.

"More like a horse, I agree," Gerry said. "Not at all in the same class—no pun intended—as Adele. But unencumbered and there's money there—very definitely, plenty of money. A calculating man could do worse. And I do begin to get the impression that Tyler Meredith was calculating, don't you?"

"The thought had begun to cross my mind," I admitted. "I'd also say he was fairly unscrupulous. You'd have to be to steal your partner's wife under his own roof."

"In the light of what we're finding out," Gerry said judiciously, "I wouldn't say he was stealing her—just borrowing her."

I thought of saying that was worse, in a way, but

decided I wouldn't give him an opportunity to call me old-fashioned again.

"Mind you," Gerry went on, "it may be six of one and half a dozen of the other. Who's to say that Endicott Zayle's intentions were strictly honourable towards his partner's invention? There must be a terrific market for someone who can come up with a sensational new anaesthetic. An international market. We mustn't allow loyalty to blind us to his possible faults just because he's our client."

"Did we ever?" I murmured. But Gerry had a point. One which brought several interesting questions to mind: Why wasn't Tyler Meredith administering his new anaesthetic himself in the test on Morgana Fane? Could it be because he hadn't known that the anaesthetic was about to be tested? Had Endicott Zayle stolen or—considering fair was fair—"borrowed" a sample of the anaesthetic to use on his difficult patient? Was that why it had had such a devastating effect on her—because he hadn't administered it in the right way? Or because his partner, suspecting professional treachery, had withheld a necessary ingredient from the formula? Something to be added at the last minute? Or had Meredith discovered what was going on, rushed in, and confronted Zayle over the supposedly dead body of Morgana Fane, been knocked out, strapped into the anaesthetic mask, and left to die in his own chair while Zayle—

While Zayle rushed to involve me? Was I supposed to be a witness to his innocence, on the presumption that he couldn't have murdered Tyler Meredith because he was with me at the time of death? Or had he thought that, by admitting to one death from the anaesthetic, he could escape suspicion on the second death? It could easily have been assumed that Tyler Meredith had discovered Morgana Fane's body and believing that his anaesthetic was a total failure—and a deadly one—committed suicide. The death of Morgana Fane would have caused such an uproar that Zayle might have hoped that the concurrent death of a fairly obscure dentist would go comparatively unnoted in the general turmoil of the situation. It had certainly floored him to discover Morgana Fane was still alive. In fact, he had been behaving oddly all along.

A thought which might be applied to *my* partner, if anyone happened along and found us. While I had been preoccupied with the deep unpleasant currents of my own thoughts, Gerry had been more active.

He had begun by applying his ear to the door in various spots, without success. He next tried the old eye-to-the-keyhole routine, but found it occupied by the key.

"Have you got a sheet of paper?" He straightened up momentarily.

"Paper?" I pulled out my pocket diary. "You can have a page out of this. Do you want to slip a note under the door?"

"That's no good." He gave me a disgusted look. "Let me have a fiver—it's bigger."

"You can't write on it so well." Dutifully, I passed him over a limp five-pound note.

"Haven't you got a better one than this?" He frowned at it critically. "I want a crisp one."

"Beggars shouldn't be choosers." But I took it

back and gave him a fresher one. I hoped that suited him—he had just run the gamut of my notecase.

"It will have to do," he said. I watched in fascination as he slid it under the door.

"I don't think you'll get her out that way," I said. "She's got plenty of money of her own, remember."

"That's not the idea." He took a thin pencil from his pocket and began prodding the keyhole with it. "I hope the key falls in the right spot," he said. "If it doesn't drop on the note, we've had it."

"We've also had it if anyone comes along and finds us," I said. I kept a nervous eye on the stairs to the lower floor. If Inspector Rennolds came up them suddenly, I wouldn't give much for our chances of seeing Villiers Street again in less than ninety days.

"Shhh, just be calm and keep your fingers crossed." Gerry probed steadily at the keyhole. "Pity we haven't a pair of eyebrow tweezers."

"Perhaps I could run down and borrow some from Adele," I suggested sarcastically. "I'm sure Inspector Rennolds wouldn't mind if we interrupted them. All in a good cause."

"Steady . . . it's coming . . ." Gerry was encouraging himself rather than me. "Easy does it now . . . easy . . . aaah . . . "

"Aha!" a voice trumpeted behind us. "There you are!" I had been so busy watching the lower stairs for Inspector Rennolds that I hadn't noticed General Sir Malcolm quietly coming down the rear stairs from his own quarters. I went rigid with shock.

"At ease!" he snapped at me, and looked down at

Gerry. He showed no surprise at finding him on his knees in front of a keyhole. It seemed to be no more than he expected. A man who wasn't in uniform at a Time Like This was capable of anything.

"I have something for you," he announced sternly to Gerry.

"Have you really?" Gerry leaped to his feet, trying to look as though he weren't dusting his knees. "I say, that's frightfully good of you. You shouldn't have bothered, you know."

"Here!" Sir Malcolm thrust something into Gerry's hands and gave him a piercing look. "Think it over!'"

Without a backward glance, he turned and marched back up the stairs to his own quarters.

"What the *hell*—?" Gerry said. "What the *bloody* hell—?"

In his hands was a long curling white feather.

Chapter 7

We heard doors opening and closing downstairs and the sound of people moving about. That meant someone might decide to come up here.

"We'd better go down," I said. "Let the Honourable Edytha worry about herself if she's caught. We don't want to be."

Trying to look innocent, we descended the stairs, Gerry twirling the feather abstractedly between his fingers. As soon as we got a few minutes alone, there were a few things I ought to try to explain to him.

"There you are," Endicott Zayle said, a pale

echo of his father. "I can take you now. Just pop in here and we'll get that tooth attended to. I'm sorry I wasn't able to manage it yesterday, but—"

I turned around, but there was no one behind me. He was looking at me and he was talking to me. There was no one else around.

"It's all right," I said. "We don't have to keep up the pretense in front of Gerry. He knows all about it. If you want a council of war, we'll have one now, but you don't have to call it by any other name. Gerry's one of the firm and we don't keep secrets from him." It would be damned hard trying to, considering the size of the office flat we shared.

"Council of war?" Zayle stared at me vaguely. "I don't know what you—"

"All right. Forget it." I was growing progressively more annoyed with him.

"But I don't understand—" His gaze wandered past me to Gerry and sharpened abruptly. "What's that you have there?"

"It seems to be a feather," Gerry said. "Your father insisted on giving it to me, but—"

"Oh, God, not again!" Zayle stepped forward and snatched away the feather, looking at it suspiciously. "It is!" he moaned. "That's from the fan Adele's grandmother carried when she was presented at Court. I thought we'd hidden it where he couldn't find it again. It costs a fortune to have it restored every time. And Adele will be furious.

"Father!" He charged past us, rushing up the stairs. "Faa-ther!"

"You know"—Gerry looked after him thoughtfully—"I never thought I'd feel sorry for a dentist, but in his case I may make an exception."

"He does seem to have quite a few problems," I agreed. No wonder he occasionally lost the thread of a conversation. If there was anything in heredity, heaven knew what kind of a memory he'd inherited from his father. The Zayle memory seemed highly selective, at best, and it would not be surprising if he chose to forget everything to do with yesterday. One might think that the continuing absence of his partner might bring it to mind; but one might also consider that, once the initial strain of caring for a double load of patients was past, his path would be considerably smoother.

"I'll see you now." The words were unpleasantly familiar; so was the voice. Once again, they seemed to be directed at me. I turned slowly.

Inspector Rennolds stood on the stairs—looking straight at me. For a fleeting moment I regretted that I had not seized my opportunity to occupy the dental chair. Then I remembered the state of the recent occupants of both dental chairs and stopped regretting it. What the patients didn't know wouldn't bother them, but it was going to be a cold day in hell before Zayle got me into either of those two chairs.

In fairness, I had to admit that Rennolds didn't look any more eager to talk to me than I was to talk to him. There was a distinct reluctance—almost a forcing himself to duty—in the way he stood aside to let me enter the room. I was relieved to notice that Gerry was following close on my heels—I didn't want to be in this alone.

Rennolds watched unhappily as we settled our-

selves on the sofa. It was really too comfortable a
room for an interrogation, but evidently, he hadn't
quite enough authority—or evidence—yet to require
us all to attend him in his office. With a sigh, he
closed the door and came over to sit in front of us.

"Is Endicott Zayle your client or your dentist?"
he began.

"It's a sort of two-way arrangement," I said.
"He does our dentistry, and we do a bit of subtle PR
for him."

"Umm, 'you scratch my back and I'll scratch
yours,' eh?"

It was an invitation I could resist. After the
silence had run on for a while, he tried again,
abruptly becoming official. "Were both of you here
yesterday?"

"No, just me." He'd have that information in
his records from the police who had been here yesterday. I took a deep breath and went the rest of the
way. "It was an emergency—one of my teeth suddenly started giving me hell. Zayle said to come
along and he'd try to fit me in." That was my story
and I was stuck all around it. I was aware of Gerry
shifting position uneasily beside me.

"I see." Impossible to tell whether the inspector
saw everything or just wanted to make it sound as
though he did. Yet there seemed to be a trace of sympathy in his tone. "And did he?"

"Did he what?" It was not a time for volunteering anything—least of all, information.

"Fit you in?"

"Actually, no. Uh—by the time he got to me,
we'd discovered—I mean, there was a call from the

reception desk to say Tyler Meredith wasn't answering his intercom and he'd patients waiting who were getting restless. We went into his surgery to see what the matter was—and we found him."

"So you didn't *actually*"—he accented the word nastily—"get any treatment yesterday?"

"Who could do any work after that? In any case, I was feeling a lot better. You know how it is—as soon as you get into the same building with the dentist, your tooth stops aching. It's practically a law of nature."

"Ummm." He was noncommittal; they weren't the laws he was called upon to enforce. "What about the others?"

"Others?"

"The other patients." He was losing his own patience; I could recognize the signs of old. It was a pity I had such an abrasive effect on him. Still, you can't win 'em all.

"Oh, yes." I brightened. "There was the Honourable Edytha Cale-Cunningham, Morgana Fane and her business manager, Sir Geoffrey Palmer—you know, the one they call in for consultations whenever there's something wrong with any Royal innards." As Inspector Rennolds grew progressively gloomier, I cheered up. "And also, the Right Honourable Mrs. Kate Halroyd, MP. All in all, a pretty influential crew."

"The C.I.D. is above influence," Rennolds said without putting over any great conviction.

"Did I say it wasn't?" I tried out an injured expression. "You asked me who was there."

"Just the same," Gerry weighed in, "I hope you've brought your best pair of kid gloves along."

"And how are all *your* teeth?" It had been a mistake to draw Rennolds's attention to himself. "Aching, too? Or did you just come along to hold your partner's hand?"

"Do you know," Gerry said, "I'm getting sick of all the insinuations around this nut hatch. If it's not one nut making them, it's another."

"And what is that supposed to mean?"

"If you haven't found out yet, all I can say is 'Congratulations'—but you will."

I noticed that the sergeant in the corner had tactfully stopped taking notes during this little slanging match, by which I gathered that Rennolds was stepping rather too far outside the official line. It emboldened me to rejoin the battle.

"In the light of what has happened," I said, somewhat pompously, "Endicott Zayle has called us in in our official capacity. Quite naturally."

"Naturally?" Rennolds's attention swung back to me. "When a man's partner dies—under his own roof—in questionable circumstances, he calls the police, he calls the doctor, he calls the undertaker, perhaps he calls the parson. But—his public relations men?"

And there he had it. I tried to keep a frozen face, not letting him see that the shot had hit home. It had not escaped my attention that, over in the corner, the sergeant had resumed note-taking with renewed zest, as though making up for lost time. I was silently cursing Zayle when Gerry made a stab at an answer.

"This is the age of information, freely given,

freely acquired. Everyone has to think of his public image. Endicott Zayle has a certain standing in the community; he recognizes his responsibility to the public to let them know what's happening." It was a good answer, but not good enough.

"And to put the best face on it?" Rennolds knew he was on to something, but not what. I wondered briefly whether I could change my story at this stage and tell him all about Morgana Fane and the false alarm that had panicked Zayle and sent him scurrying to Perkins & Tate.

"Let's face it"—changing my mind, I tossed in a tentative towel—"the whole family is pretty eccentric."

"I'd wondered when we were going to come to something like that." The sergeant's transcript would never do full justice to the inspector's interviews—there was no way of writing in the shades of meaning underlying every phrase. "I may say that I thought Mrs. Zayle a very well-balanced and sensible woman."

It hadn't been Adele I'd been thinking of—at least, not primarily. I was interested in the inspector's opinion of her, though. It meant she had kept her temper under control while she was talking to him. If he'd ever seen her the way Gerry and I had, neither "well-balanced" nor "sensible" were words that would spring readily to mind.

"You're going to tell me," he prophesied inaccurately, "that a wife can't testify against her husband. That isn't so. A wife cannot be *forced* to give evidence against her husband, but, if she wishes to, she can. Mrs. Zayle wishes to."

"Does that ever go down well with a jury, though?" Gerry asked. "Smacks a bit too much of vindictiveness and settling old scores. Sort of thing that leaves a bad taste in the mouth. English juries especially don't like it."

It was another good try, but I thought we were getting a bit too far advanced.

"Who said anything about juries?" I blithely ignored the fact that the inspector had introduced the subject of testimony. "I'm sure we've all noticed that Mrs. Zayle has her own ax to grind." And after honing a sharp enough edge, the spot she was aiming it at was her husband's neck. "She couldn't be considered an unprejudiced witness. Apart from which, she wasn't even here at the time her—um, fiancé—died. I'd say any contribution she might make would be pretty worthless, all things considered."

"We *intend* to consider everything." I consoled myself with the thought that he wouldn't have kept his attention away from me indefinitely. "For instance, Mrs. Zayle tells me that her father-in-law will support all her contentions."

I wondered if he would have been so indiscreet if his dislike for me hadn't triggered him into it. I noticed that the sergeant had stopped taking notes again and his pen was jittering unhappily just above his notebook. Was it an indication that the inspector was way out of line—or was it just a very well-rehearsed double act to knock witnesses off their guard?

"Try telling me," Inspector Rennolds said triumphantly, "that General Sir Malcolm Zayle won't impress a jury!"

"Oh, he'll impress them all right," I admitted. "Tell me," I probed cautiously, "have you had a talk with the General yet?"

"Not yet."

I hadn't thought so when he'd spoken with so much confidence.

"But we'll be questioning him soon. Mrs. Zayle tells me that he was here all day yesterday. That means he might be helpful at narrowing down the actual time."

"Oh, I'm sure he will be," I said. "He'll probably put it at either 1914 or 1940."

"As late as that?" Automatically, Inspector Rennolds glanced at his watch. "We thought it was around sixteen hundred. Still, the autopsy report will give us a better indication."

I didn't bother to tell him I wasn't talking in terms of the twenty-four-hour clock. What is life without surprises? He was due for a beauty when he questioned General Sir Malcolm Zayle. It would be a shame to spoil it in advance.

On the other hand—I discovered a new worry— General Sir Malcolm Zayle actually *might* make an impressive witness. For all the wrong reasons. His defence of his son could be more damning than his daughter-in-law's accusations, precisely because he was so certain that his son had done the correct thing and that any right-minded minion of society ought to recognize the fact. I wondered if there were any possible way to yank Sir Malcolm into the proper decade of the twentieth century before he did more damage with that time-warp displacement of his. Perhaps a psychiatrist? Perhaps a good knock on the head? Perhaps a push downstairs?

Which brought us back to Adele. If she had discovered that she wasn't Tyler Meredith's only fiancée, into what revenge might that red-haired temper have led her?

"By the way," I said, "have you interviewed the Honourable Edytha yet?"

"Who?" Over in the corner, the sergeant recorded these seemingly unloaded words with relief. He couldn't show up with a blank pad when an interview had been indicated.

"The Honourable Edytha Cale-Cunningham. She was here yesterday. Downstairs, in the waiting room with the others. She was—" Discretion abruptly set in; the valiant could look out for themselves. "She was Tyler Meredith's patient." Let her tell him the erstwhile-happy tidings herself. I began to have the strong feeling that I'd said too much already.

"She's on the list to be interviewed," he assured me, with an emphasis that instantly made me doubt it. He'd been having the whole case handed to him on a platter—and come to think of it, Adele would have made an excellent Salome—and he wasn't too interested in clouding the issue.

"In the absence of a solicitor"—I decided to drag a few more clouds down to obscure matters—"I would like to protest . . ." I hesitated there, not being sure quite what I ought to protest, but it was a good line.

"You *don't* want me to interview Miss Cale-Cunningham?" Rennolds was beginning to look faintly groggy. So was the sergeant, still struggling to keep up with the turns of the conversation. "You just suggested that I should do so."

The telephone began to ring and the sergeant lunged for it, delighted to be presented with a situation he could cope with.

"I protest"—I went on, decided it was time to make some noises like a public relations person—"your taking the word of a neurotic and unreliable woman who demonstrably hates her husband—"

The sergeant put the receiver down on the table and came over to murmur something into the inspector's ear. Rennolds nodded.

"I protest your even considering that our client might have had anything to do with—whatever has happened here."

"Yes?" Rennolds said. "Why don't you go paint some banners and have a march? I'll speak to you again later." He stood up. "Meanwhile, I have a private call coming through here."

"I protest," I continued as he herded us toward the door, "this harassment of an honest and upright citizen. A man dedicated to the cause of suffering humanity. Wherever you find your criminals, you don't find them among the humanitarian professional class."

"I'll make a note of that," he said absently, opening the door and seeing us into the hall.

"A dentist!" Emboldened more by the thought of getting away from him than by any success I thought I was having, I kept firing parting shots. "A man whose life's work is relieving pain and—"

"There's one thing you might remember." He

paused in closing the door. "Everyone else seems to have forgotten it."

"What's that?" I asked cautiously. I knew I wasn't going to like the answer, and I didn't.

"Just remember"—his lips twitched upward in a grimace that was more a wolfish snarl than a smile— "some people think Crippen was a dentist."

Chapter 8

"As a thought for the day," Gerry said, moodily regarding the closed door, "that may inspire the inspector, but it doesn't do a thing for me."

"Frankly, it depresses me," I said. "It was one thing to quietly marshal the possible evidence against the client between ourselves, but it was unnerving to discover how far along the same path the law was racing ahead of us."

"Let's get out of here," Gerry said abruptly.

"The inspector didn't say we could go," I reminded him.

"He didn't say we couldn't." Gerry was ever the optimist.

"Perhaps we could go back to the waiting room for half an hour or so. Out of sight, out of mind. Then if he doesn't call us back, we can leave and have the excuse that we waited for some time, but had to get back to the office."

"Good thinking," Gerry said. "Let's get out of sight right now." Without waiting for my answer, he started downstairs and I plunged after him. I didn't intend to be found in the hall by myself if the inspector should end his telephone conversation quickly and come looking for us.

I discovered it was old home week as we walked into the waiting room—and I didn't like it one little bit. It looked like the gathering of the clans—if you presupposed that there had been some great clan tragedy.

Yesterday's cast was now complete, with Mrs. Kate Halroyd, MP, Morgana Fane and her business manager, all sitting in various attitudes of dejection around the waiting room. Even the newcomers—who were, presumably, today's appointments—seemed infected by the general air of gloom.

It's not that anyone expects a dentist's waiting room to have an air of jollification and general merriment, but this place was as cheerful as a wake. All that was missing was the corpse.

I immediately wished I hadn't thought of that.

Even Gerry seemed subdued. He followed me to an unoccupied corner and sat down without attempting to disperse any sweetness and light. A sure sign—when there were celebrities present—that he had subconsciously tested the emotional temperature of the water and decided that it was better to imitate an invisible jellyfish rather than a large frog in a small pond. He didn't often come to that conclusion. It added to my uneasiness.

When he picked up a three-year-old copy of *Country Life* and immersed himself in it, my worst fears were realized. To all intents and purposes, he was no longer with us and—with his unfailing sense of occasion—that meant all hell was ready to break loose.

I picked up a rather later issue of *Punch* and tried to follow his example, but was doomed before I started. I had carelessly let my gaze cross that of Mrs. Kate Halroyd. She leaned forward and fixed me with an accusing eye.

"*You* were here yesterday," she breathed.

"Er, well, actually . . . yes," I admitted.

This promptly riveted the attention of the other occupants of the waiting room upon me. I smiled apologetically and tried to look as though I were dying to plunge into *Punch*. It didn't work for a moment.

"That's right," she said. "You took my place—and I—I went back to the House."

"Well, you *did* rather insist, you know," I defended feebly. "I never intended to." I glanced sideways at Gerry for help, but it was no use. He was deep in *Country Life*—he had never seen me before in his life.

"If only I had been up there," she mourned. "If only I had kept my appointment—"

"Honestly"—I tried to comfort her—"there was nothing anyone could do. He'd been—er—it had happened quite awhile earlier. You couldn't have made any difference—"

"But I wasn't there," she said. "And so, I'll never know. There might have been something—"

"We did everything we could." I'll never know whether I was comforting her or rubbing salt in the wound. "Believe me, there was nothing—"

"You're trying to be kind." She gave me a brief, tight smile that disclosed those yellowed, crumbling teeth again and gazed off into the distance.

Unfortunately, none of the others joined her in studying the distant vistas; they were all too busy staring at me. I began to feel like a sideshow exhibit. I was going to be a bitter disappointment to them at any moment by failing to turn and disclose gills or feathers in unexpected places. I tried outstaring them, but I was outnumbered and it didn't work. I took the only other option open to me and gazed off into space myself.

"Yes," she said, "you're very kind." She lowered her voice, which did nothing to diminish its carrying power—I've heard West End actresses who couldn't project so well at full power as she did with her lowered voice. It seemed to curl into every corner of the room and echo back at us off the walls.

"I shall never forgive myself. It was my place— my duty—to be there."

"No, really," I said. My own voice was almost

inaudible, even to me, but as everyone else in the
waiting room seemed to be holding their breath in
order not to miss any of the dialogue, I was bitterly
aware that it wasn't inaudible enough. "You mustn't
blame yourself. Anyone could be excused for wanting
to skip a dental appointment. And you were trying to
do a kindness to someone else—to me. You have
nothing to reproach yourself about."

"You don't understand." She turned her dark,
brooding eyes upon me. "You don't know all the circumstances. You see, I was engaged to Tyler
Meredith. It was a secret at present, but—after we
worked out a few difficulties—we were going to be
married."

Over my own gulp of astonishment, I heard
Country Life hit the floor. Gerry retrieved it quickly,
but gave up the pretense of being absorbed in it. He
joined the rest of our breathless audience, goggling
shamelessly, ears all but flapping.

"Yes," she said. "There's no point in keeping it
secret now." She was oblivious to her listeners.
Rather, I revised my opinion, she seemed to accept
them as right and natural. As though she were so
accustomed to living her life in full view of the mul-
titudes that they hardly registered on her con-
sciousness anymore.

"He was at the threshold of a brilliant career in
public service." It looked as though we were in for a
recitation of all the departed's virtues. Well, perhaps it made her feel a bit better.

"I know," I said. "He was developing a wonderful new anaesthetic which was going to be of great benefit to the public."

"Not that." She moved both head and hands in an impatient gesture of negation. "Oh, I know it's wonderful—it was to be his parting gift to a profession which had served him, but which really meant little more to him than the stages he began his life on. His *real* future had nothing to do with *this*." She encompassed the waiting room, the surgery, the entire building, with contempt in her tone.

Across the room, I was aware of Morgana Fane regarding us intently. She leaned forward, one elbow on the arm of her chair, her hand cradling her jaw— my own jaw winced in sympathy—and watched us as though we were a command performance convened for her own special entertainment. Except that she didn't seem very entertained. More probably, we were a welcome diversion to take her mind off her dental problems and the ordeal waiting for her upstairs in the surgery. I wondered if she was here again today on the principle of getting straight back on the horse after having fallen off—it couldn't be easy for her to get back into that chair where she had had such an unpleasant experience. (I made a mental bet that she was settling for ordinary procaine this time around.) Was that why her manager was with her again—for moral support? Or was he just a glorified chauffeur, standing by to take her on to her next photo session?

Or—another, nastier, thought suddenly occurred to me—had the police sent for those who had been here yesterday, in order to facilitate their inquiries?

Could they do that? Was it only because I was already here that I hadn't been sent for? I decided I didn't really want to know the answers to those questions and tried to stop thinking about them. Even though this meant I had to return my attention to the still-voluble mourner beside me.

". . . truly brilliant career opening out before him. I was so certain of it, I was going to give up my seat to him—after we were married, of course."

I rolled with that punch and let my mind wander. She took a terrible picture, I realized, looking at her. In fact, she must be one of our least photogenic MPs. The ghastly hats she persisted in wearing every time she was photographed didn't help, either. Nor did her habit of never smiling—although I'd seen the reason for it when she first smiled at me yesterday—do anything to soften the grim visage the cameras recorded.

In person, and without a hat, she looked softer and more attractive. It was too bad she hadn't met a sympathetic photographer—

I pulled myself together abruptly. This was no time to be thinking of business. At least, not new business. We had quite as much as we could manage trying to keep our devious dentist out of the clutches of the law. Once that was accomplished—*if* it was accomplished—we could worry about new clients.

". . . brought me here today," she was saying.

"Yes?" I tried to look as though I had been paying rapt attention.

"I wanted to collect a few things from his flat— just little personal things. Nothing valuable. They wouldn't mean a thing to anyone else. But, I thought—if I might go up and—"

You and half of London. But I couldn't say that. I nodded, with what I hoped was a suitably understanding expression. As long as she didn't look at Gerry, we were all right. His bemused expression would have given the game away—or at least, told her there was a game.

"I really must"—she took a deep breath and stood up decisively—"go and speak to Mr. Zayle about it now. I—I just wanted to sit down for a moment and—and gather myself together, as it were."

"Of course, but"—I felt I had to warn her—"I think you'll have to speak to someone other than Mr. Zayle. There's still an investigation going on and the policeman in charge of it is upstairs in the Zayle living room. I believe you'll have to get his permission before you do anything about the Meredith flat."

"I see." She drew in her breath thoughtfully.

"Just tell him everything you've told me," I said encouragingly. "Especially the part about being secretly engaged." That would give Rennolds some food for thought—enough to choke him, if we were lucky.

"Tchk!" She made an impatient exclamation with her tongue. "I haven't much time to spare. There's an important debate coming up—I must get back to the House. It will probably mean a division—*and* an all-night sitting."

"Tell that to the inspector. He'll understand." I smiled reassuringly to her as she went out the door.

Then I became aware that Gerry was signaling to me urgently. I, too, felt that a corridor conference was strongly indicated and nodded. We gave our MP time enough to clear the stairs and be out of our way, then wandered out of the waiting room with a vague indifference which probably fooled no one.

Certainly not Morgana Fane. She was watching us with a curious expression, and for a nasty moment, I thought she was going to follow us out and declare herself in on whatever we were doing. Fortunately, she had second thoughts—if she'd ever had the first thought—and we found ourselves alone in the corridor.

"Well," I said, "wait until Rennolds hears the rest of the tales of the lovelorn. That ought to change his mind about Zayle." I couldn't help gloating a bit. I'm as law-abiding as the next one, but I felt that Rennolds deserved any problems he got.

"Mm-hmm." Gerry was still bemused, trying to follow the workings of a mind he was beginning to admire. "It's a pity we did our trading with the wrong partner. That Meredith was a genius. Do you see how perfectly he planned things? The Honourable Edytha's money, backing a political career handed to him on a platter by the Right Honourable MP, and with Adele in the background for a spot of luscious crumpet when he felt like a pastry."

There was no mistaking it, Gerry's tone was openly envious.

"Do you realize Tyler Meredith was on the verge of pioneering new frontiers in bigamy?"

"He didn't get away with it," I reminded Gerry, bringing him down to earth sharply.

"No, he didn't, did he?" He brightened slightly. "I guess I'd better stick to the love 'em and leave 'em routine. It has its drawbacks, but—"

"But it's healthier," I finished for him.

"True, only too true." He shook his head sadly. "Birds get very upset about little things. Each one likes to think she's the only one in the nest—let alone wearing the wedding ring. Whichever one of Meredith's birds found out about the other two—"

"The hot-tempered Adele." I cast my vote promptly, unable to forget the way she had tried to push her husband into the path of the oncoming train. "That woman would do anything."

"On impulse, yes," Gerry said. "But I'm not so sure about long-distance planning. Remember, she has an alibi for the past week. She was with friends at the seaside."

"Alibis can be staged," I argued, "and any true friend would do a bit of lying in a good cause."

"A good cause?" Gerry raised his eyebrows.

"If the friend was another woman—who also didn't approve of bigamy."

"Only too true again," Gerry admitted sadly. "The best of birds is likely to have a very wonky view of morality."

"I suppose you can't really blame them," I said. "They just see things differently from us."

"Now my money," Gerry said, "is on the

Honourable Edytha. It's always those tall, thin, high-strung ones you've got to watch. They're overbred, or something, like horses. One minute they're perfectly all right, the next minute they're trying to knock your head off charging under a low branch, or trying to break your leg brushing you off against a fence. If I'd ever had a horse," he added thoughtfully, "that showed as much white to its eye as the Honourable Edytha, I'd have shot it before it got a chance to do any damage. Some creatures you just can't trust."

It was a good argument, but I doubted that it would hold up in a court of law. "Maybe," I said, "but she strikes me as too timid to be violent. How about the Right Honourable MP? Now there"—I warmed to the idea—"is a woman I would put nothing past."

"Neither would the Opposition," Gerry said. "Even though she's been known to work very well on committees."

"What do you mean?"

"The hardest thing to bring off in bigamy," Gerry said, as though he'd thought deeply about the subject, "is keeping the ladies apart. Suppose Meredith didn't manage it. The wronged ladies could have formed a conspiracy for revenge and drawn straws or something for the one who'd actually do the deed. Then the others got to work and manufactured three solid alibis." He looked into space thoughtfully. "I wouldn't be surprised if a conspiracy like that were pretty nearly undetectable. So long as none of them broke under the strain."

"That's a bloodcurdling thought." I felt as though the temperature had plummeted a good thirty degrees, although the thermostat on the wall beside me continued to register a perfectly respectable reading of 70°F. "But it could have worked. Edytha and Kate alibied each other in the waiting room. Sir Geoffrey admitted he'd only been there half an hour. It might depend on just when Tyler Meredith died. How long it took, I mean. One or both could have slipped past the receptionist, knocked Meredith out, strapped the mask over his face, and gone back to the waiting room—trusting to luck that no one would go into the surgery in time to rescue him."

"Even if he was discovered in time," Gerry said, "they didn't run much of a risk. Could he bring any sort of charges? He'd have to admit what had driven them to it—and I'm not sure it isn't the kind of crime that draws a prison sentence. At any rate, you've got to admit society frowns on bigamy."

"Whichever one did it," I said, "no one could deny she had sufficient provocation. Quite probably, no jury would convict her. Not if there were any other women on it—and any decent QC would see to it that there were."

"Provocation, indeed," Gerry said.

"You've got to admit Tyler Meredith brought it on himself. After all, he was planning to betray—" Was that quite the right word? I tried again. "He plotted to *use*—" That didn't seem the mot juste, either. "Er . . ." I floundered desperately.

"The situation reminds me," Gerry said solemnly, "of a classic American newspaper legend. It happened back in the innocent days. There was a sensational court case featuring a dentist accused of rape.

"Naturally, no respectable newspaper could print such a word in those days. Not even when the jury found the accused guilty as charged. The brightest sparks of one of the leading newspapers cudgeled their brains late into the night trying to come up with a lead fit for the delicate sensibilities of their readers." He paused.

"And?" I prompted.

"They finally headlined it," he said, " 'Dentist Fills Wrong Cavity.' "

Chapter 9

We were carelessly standing with our backs to the stairs; a mistake I became aware of when a sudden clatter of onrushing heels sounded unnervingly close behind me. I half expected, as I turned, to face the Honourable Edytha, rushing away from memories which had suddenly threatened to overcome her.

Instead, I was nose-to-flaring-nostril with Adele. Chin high, haughty, and imperious, she defied me to remain blocking her path. I wouldn't have been surprised if she had commanded, "Out of the way, peasant!" I stepped away hastily. There was no doubt about it—if we had been in a Roman amphitheatre, Adele's thumb would have been turned down.

However, she did her best to twitch the corners of her mouth into a smile. It wasn't a very good smile, but one had to applaud the obvious effort.

"I—I'm sorry," she said, sidling past. "I—I just feel I need a breath of fresh air." It was so unconvincing it was almost original.

"Then, allow me." Gerry crossed and swung the front door open for her with a flourish. It wasn't until he had closed it behind her and turned back to me that a thoughtful look occupied his face.

"Did you notice anything just then?" he asked.

"Anything?"

"That thing she was carrying. Was it one of those large-size handbags, or one of those small-size overnight cases?"

"I don't know," I said. I might have added that I didn't want to know. We had enough problems. If Adele decided to go back to her friends on the coast, or to go home to mother, it wasn't for us to worry about. I felt Zayle could only be congratulated—but would he see it that way?

"I wonder whether we should have let her go." Gerry was determined to worry. "The inspector won't like it."

"How could we have stopped her? And why should we have? We've nothing to do with the police. If the inspector wants to keep people cooped up, he should have put a policeman on the door. So far as we're concerned, that was the client's wife and she wanted to go out. Were we supposed to bring her down with a flying tackle and carry her back up-stairs?"

I was working myself into a fine state of righteous indignation. It sounded like a pretty solid argument—but would the inspector view it that way?

"That's right." Gerry, at least, was willing to view it that way. "It isn't up to us to keep track of his suspects. In fact, so far as I'm concerned, we haven't even seen her this afternoon."

"That may be the best story," I agreed. "Besides, we aren't certain she's decamped."

"No, but I wouldn't like to take any bets on it."

Neither would I. The experience had taught me a lesson, though, and I faced the stairs as we resumed our conference. I wasn't going to be caught off guard again.

That was how I happened to see Penny as she darted out of the surgery and down into the loo on the landing of the stairs, pausing only to give us a cheerful wave. There was nothing unusual in that.

What was unusual was the way in which Zayle almost immediately emerged from the surgery and pussyfooted up the stairs. His manner was distinctly furtive. What's more, he didn't make a return journey. I wondered if he had his own set of keys to his partner's quarters. It would hardly be surprising—it was his house, after all.

"What do you think—?" Although Gerry had his back to the stairs and hadn't seen a thing, he came to the crux of the situation with his usual sixth sense. "What do you think the dear departed kept in that flat? I mean, it's positively unnatural the way all

those birds want to get in there and remove sou-
venirs. Do you suppose he had a collection of nude
photos of them? Or do you suppose he peddled drugs
in his spare time and they want to get their hands on
what's left, now that the source of supply has been
cut off?"

"What spare time?" I asked. "Running all those
women simultaneously couldn't have left him with
much. It's a wonder he had enough time left to work
on any formulas." And that was a thought—perhaps they were looking for the formula. Certainly, it
was the most likely thing for Zayle to be searching
for.

During the thoughtful silence, the door of the
waiting room opened. Models can have a curiously
extinguished look in off-duty moments when the
cameras aren't clicking. Morgana Fane had this now
as she slipped past us with a demure smile. The
most vivid proclamation of life about her emanated
from the glittering op art medallion around her
throat. It seemed to whirl and pulse with a life of its
own. It made me feel off balance and slightly dizzy
just to look at it. It was the sort of thing she would
have picked up on one of her working trips to the
States. Undoubtedly, it was the next fad she was
about to launch here. It ought to make the costume
jewellery industry very happy—and the manufac-
turers of aspirin tablets delirious with joy.

She went up the stairs, heading purposefully
for the landing. As she reached it, the door opened
and Penny came out while she went in.

"You know"—Gerry had turned to follow

Morgana's progress up the stairs—"there's something funny there."

"Considering her reputation," I agreed, "she seems strangely subdued these days. Perhaps it's a side effect of the new anaesthetic."

"In which case," Gerry said, "a double fortune awaits the stuff's debut on the open market. If it can subdue her, it can sell on its secondary properties alone."

"On the other hand, she may be practicing for her new station in life," I reflected. "Or perhaps her brush with the Valley of the Shadow has shaken her enough to turn over a new leaf."

"How could it when she doesn't realize how close she was?"

"Perhaps her subconscious realizes it. Anyway—"

"Attention!" We snapped into it automatically at the sharp command.

Intent on analysing the situation with Gerry, I had been neglecting my vigil on the staircase. Now General Sir Malcolm Zayle stood before us, carrying out inspection.

"Still no uniforms?" he demanded harshly of Gerry.

"Neither has he—" Gerry was reduced to pointing at me.

"That's different," Sir Malcolm told him. "His uniform is on the way. I know all about him—he's Geoffrey's adjutant. Good man, Geoffrey." He nodded to me. "You'll learn a lot from him."

"I feel I already have—sir," I said. I felt quite grateful to Sir Geoffrey, whose timely intervention had saved me from the sort of problem poor Gerry kept encountering with the General.

"At ease," Sir Malcolm said.

I relaxed, while Gerry tried to look as though he had never snapped to attention in the first place. General Sir Malcolm continued to survey us both.

"Mission tonight," he said. "Might be dangerous. I need a volunteer."

Gerry silently took two brisk steps backward, leaving me in the vanguard. Sir Malcolm nodded approval.

"Good man," he said. "I knew I could count on you."

I smiled weakly, resolving that, if the dangerous mission had anything to do with dentistry, I was going to go over the hill—and let them bring on their firing squad.

"Right!" He nodded again. "Report to my quarters in two hours." His mouth softened into almost a smile. "Mufti will do." He turned and marched upstairs.

"It's all right for some," Gerry said. "It's lucky I haven't any ambition to be the sweetheart of the regiment, or I might start getting jealous."

"Thank you for volunteering me," I said. "I must do something nice for *you* someday."

"Now, now, what can you expect from a white-feather man? Go and serve your country, like a nice little hero. Perhaps you'll win a VC."

I glanced at my watch. "Whatever this mission is, I'm not going to face it on an empty stomach. Let's slide out and get a drink and a sandwich before I march to face the foe."

• • •

"Have fun with the Dawn Patrol," Gerry said as we left the pub. "You never know your luck—you might run into Mata Hari or Tokyo Rose."

I was relieved to find the Zayle hallway empty, the waiting room deserted, the receptionist gone for the night. My footsteps seemed to thud against the carpet as I climbed the stairs. I might have been moving through an empty building; no sounds came from any of the living quarters, and only the faintest gurgle of running water from the surgeries where water perpetually squirted round the inside of the china spittoons beside the chairs, ready to whisk from sight the next expectoration of saliva, blood, and fragments of tooth. I shuddered and quickened my pace.

A sliver of light beneath the door leading to General Sir Malcolm's quarters was the first sign of life I had seen in the entire building. I hurled myself toward it thankfully and rapped on that door, telling myself it was silly to let my nerves play tricks on me. There was nothing sinister about the house; it was the surgery and living quarters of a perfectly respectable dentist, whose partner had met with an unfortunate accident. There was nothing sinister about it.

If I told myself that often enough, I might believe it. As it was, I was delighted when the door swung open and Sir Malcolm's tall, military figure was silhouetted by the light behind. I beamed at him, then realized this might not be the proper attitude for one of the ranks. I wiped the smile off my face quickly and saluted.

"Good evening, sir."

"At ease." He checked his watch. "You're early. I like that. Eager. Ready for action. You're a good lad. Come in."

I followed him into his quarters. They were military to the point of being Spartan. The only personal touch consisted of two photographs, both of extraordinarily beautiful women. I recalled reading that he had been married twice. One beauty was dressed in the costume of the 1916 era; the other in the more familiar clothes of the late 1930s. I wondered whether that was the key—or half of it—to the wanderings of his mind, continually harking back to the two eras when he had been triumphant in battle and in love. The days of glory—you could hardly blame him for not wanting to relinquish them.

"Through here," he said, leading me through a monastic cell with a single divan and through French windows onto the roof. "Over here."

It was a small shed which seemed to have been built as an afterthought sometime after the original roof had been topped and semilandscaped. He opened the door and motioned me inside.

"Just help me with these things. We'll get them out and ready for action, eh?"

Two buckets of water, two buckets of sand, a stirrup pump, a heavy blanket, a couple of chairs, a pair of binoculars, a chemical fire extinguisher—we took them out of the shed and arranged them at strategic points around the roof. I had gone into such a daze that I scarcely flinched when he suddenly plonked an ARP helmet on my head.

"Sit down," he said, taking one of the chairs for

himself. I sank into the other one thankfully, wondering what was coming next. I hoped he didn't start his own fires to help his fantasies along.

He shot me a sly, penetrating look from those piercing blue eyes, which abruptly unsettled me. Did he realize then that the whole procession of his days was an elaborate charade? Was he behaving like this as some way of revenging himself on his family for something he'd imagined they had—or hadn't—done to him? Old people sometimes got like that.

"Think I'm mad, don't you?" he demanded suddenly.

"No more than most." I shrugged. It was probably true. In PR, you seldom met the best-balanced portion of the citizenry. It stood to reason. When you get people with so much—or so little—ego that they demand a constant flow of their own names and doings through the columns, you're more likely to be dealing with raving monomaniacs than with Nature's gentlemen or gentlewomen. Sometimes you wonder whether they doubt their own existence without the constant proof before them in black and white.

"Method in my madness," he admitted, looking almost shy. "Knew a sporting young blood like you wouldn't volunteer for a mission unless there was danger involved. I was like that myself. Knew the boring jobs had to be done, but didn't want to be the one to do them."

"You mean," I said, gesturing at the equipment deployed around the roof, "*this* is the mission?"

"Fire watching," he said. "Has to be done. No one else wants to know. They think just because the Jerries haven't been over for the past few nights, they won't be coming again."

"Silly of them," I said absently, wondering if I was expected to remain on this roof all night. That blanket didn't look any too warm. Apart from which, I had the nasty suspicion that it was intended only for smothering possible incendiaries, and not for human comfort.

"I knew you'd see it my way." Sir Malcolm hesitated and made an apologetic gesture. "You don't mind my little deception, then? Letting you think there was going to be excitement, danger?"

"No, no, of course not, sir." I tried to look suitably chagrined. "I understand."

"There's every good chance they'll come over tonight," he offered. "They've been lying doggo too long. And when they come, they'll make up for the nights they've missed. There'll be bombs falling all around us yet."

I realized he was trying to cheer me up. "Quite likely, sir," I agreed.

"Of course," he said thoughtfully, "our boys do a magnificent job turning them back at the coast. But it's just a question of time until some get through— law of averages. A few are bound to, sooner or later."

"Yes, sir." I tried to look happy at this view of the situation. It was a mistake; it seemed to egg him on to visualizing fresh terrors to inspire me.

"I'm an old campaigner, m' boy, and sometimes you can feel things in your bones. You'll know the feeling, too, after your first few sorties in enemy territory. I tell you, something's going to happen tonight. I know it."

"Yes, sir." What worried me was that *I* was beginning to feel it, too. A campaign is a campaign, and I'd back a few years in PR against any active service, any day. We were both battle-scarred veterans. I wished I didn't have the feeling that we were about to gain a few more scars.

"There it goes!" He sprang to his feet. So did I.

A high-pitched shriek rose and fell around us. I found myself automatically scanning the sky and longing, for a wild moment, to snatch the binoculars from Sir Malcolm's hands and use them myself.

After a long unreal minute, common sense reasserted itself and I remembered which decade we were really living in. I pulled myself together and listened to the agonizing sound carefully. It was the ear-splitting variety which seemed to come from everywhere and nowhere, but after another minute, I located it.

"Downstairs!" I said. Sir Malcolm was still training his binoculars on the horizon. I took a step closer and shouted in his ear.

"It's coming from downstairs. A woman screaming. We ought to investigate—sir."

"Screaming?" Sir Malcolm lowered the glasses, his eyes shining with the light of battle. It seemed that any direct action would suffice.

"Downstairs!" he ordered. "Immediately!" He charged for the open door, enemy aircraft forgotten. He even went down the stairs two at a time.

Adele was in the first-floor hallway, her back to the wall beside the open door of Tyler Meredith's surgery. The terrible high-pitched wail was coming from her.

Endicott Zayle was standing beside her. He had obviously just reached her side and was trying ineffectually to quiet her. Sir Geoffrey Palmer was coming up the stairs from the ground floor, having evidently just arrived, and we all converged on Adele at once with various theories.

"Slap her face!" Sir Malcolm ordered. "Only thing to do when they're hysterical."

"Father, please," Endicott said. "Adele, please—"

"Here—" Sir Geoffrey shouldered his way through. He, after all, was the medical man. "Now, what's the matter?"

Adele gulped for breath; the sudden silence was astonishing. That soprano shriek seemed to have been sounding in our ears since time began. She gulped air again, but still didn't seem able to speak.

"Perhaps a glass of water—" I said.

"NOO-OO-oo—" My innocent suggestion seemed to have set her off again. We all glanced at one another helplessly.

I stood there, trying to comprehend her strange antipathy to water and gradually became aware of a certain squidginess about the carpet at my feet. In the uneasy silence, as Sir Geoffrey managed to calm her again, the sound of running, gurgling, splashing water was clear from the surgery.

I let these facts seep in for a minute, then moved to the open door of the surgery reluctantly. In the silence, the others watched me.

The hall carpet was wet. Sopping, in fact, just outside the surgery door, where a small tidal wave moved across the polished linoleum to meet the carpet at the threshold. The pool of water covered the entire surgery floor. How long, I wondered, had the water been leaking? Some considerable time, probably, to get everything this innundated. I tried to follow the sound of splashing to discover where the leak was originating.

My gaze moved slowly across the rippling floor to the source of the splashing water beside the dental chair. It wasn't a leak.

Water spilled over the top of the china spittoon, flooding over the edge of the blocked bowl.

A woman slumped, half-in and half-out of the dental chair, twisted awkwardly, so that her face was hidden in the basin.

I began to wade across the room, my hackles rising. She was too motionless, her face too submerged in that bubbling spittoon. The amount of water lapping around my feet told me that she had been there for a considerable length of time.

I heard the splashing as the others started across the room after me. From the doorway, Adele began to shriek again. How far into the room had she ventured? Far enough to see what I could see now and know that there was no hope for the victim?

Her hair covered the base of her skull, but I knew that there must be a bruise beneath it. Otherwise, the Honourable Edytha would never have sat calmly in the dental chair and allowed someone to ram her head so far into the china spittoon that she could drown—practically in the proverbial cup of water.

"Where's that inspector?" Sir Geoffrey asked abruptly.

"He left some time ago," Endicott said.

In the background, General Sir Malcolm Zayle spoke bitterly for all of us. "Why," he demanded, "is there never a policeman around when you want one?"

Chapter 10

"There was no question of the kiss of life, or any-thing like that," I told Gerry next morning. "She was gone. I think we all knew that, even without Sir Geoffrey's confirmation."

It probably wasn't the best subject for breakfast table conversation, but that didn't appear to bother Gerry. This was the first chance I'd had to bring him up-to-date. By the time the police had been summoned and had carried out their preliminary inquiries, it was the early hours of the morning before I got home.

Pandora was annoyed at me and showed her disapproval of such alley-cat hours by sitting over on Gerry's side of the desk, which served us as a table outside of office hours. Also, Gerry was generally a more careless eater. He proved this now by looking across the desk at me, neglecting his boiled egg.

"I suppose," he said hopefully, "it couldn't have been suicide? In the same dental chair as her dead lover and all that? She might have decided she didn't want to go on without him and—"

"Not a chance," I said. "We had to break the bowl to get her head out, she'd been jammed in so tightly. And the drainpipe had been blocked—with those cotton rolls dentists stuff into your mouth—to make sure the bowl stayed full of enough water to do the job. She couldn't possibly have—"

"Please—" Gerry waved his spoon in the air in protest. I was getting too graphic.

Pandora took the opportunity to dip into Gerry's egg.

"*Oi!*" He came back to reality with an indignant shout. "Get out of there! What do you think you're doing?"

Pandora backed away, licking egg yolk from her nose. She knew what she was doing—she was enjoying an extra bit of breakfast. It always tasted better when it was stolen.

"Look at that!" Gerry said, aggrieved. He carefully scraped the surface of the egg with his spoon and held it out to Pandora. "Now you can just eat that bit, too. Who do you suppose wants your leavings?"

Pandora licked the spoon meticulously, delighted

with her luck. When it was shining, Gerry withdrew it. "That's better," he said. "Who do you think wants to eat something after you've left your germs all over it?"

He then plunged the spoon back into the egg and transferred a large segment to his own mouth, with gusto. Pandora sat there alertly, waiting her next opportunity for another dip.

He didn't seem to notice the anomaly of his behavior—and I didn't bother to point it out. They were both perfectly happy and we were all undoubtedly impervious to each other's germs by this time.

"The thing is"—I was still intent on my own thoughts—"Adele claimed she'd been out for a walk and had just come back. She said she noticed water coming from the surgery as she got to the head of the stairs. She opened the door, looked inside—and began screaming."

"Quite rightly, too," Gerry said. "I've always maintained that there are moments when a woman ought to be allowed a scream or two. That was quite definitely one of them."

"Maybe so," I said, "but her story doesn't—" I stopped. I'd been going to say "hold water," but on second thought, it was gong to be a long while before I tossed the word "water" around lightly again. I'd seen the Honourable Edytha's drowned face when they freed it from the overflowing bowl.

"There was something wrong," I finished instead.

"Such as?" Gerry raised an eyebrow. For a moment, he nearly raised his spoon, but he noticed Pandora's head cock alertly just in time.

"She was wearing her coat," I said slowly. "And perhaps she *had* just come in, but . . ."

"But what?" I had Gerry's complete attention now, and Pandora dived into his egg again. With a resigned shrug, he pushed the plate toward her, so that she could eat it comfortably without stretching. "It was nearly finished, anyway," he said. "What about Adele?"

"She wasn't carrying anything," I said. "That big bag we'd both noticed—she didn't have it. And it wasn't dropped at the head of the stairs or the door of the surgery, or anything. She just plain didn't have it."

"Meaning," he said thoughtfully, "she'd been back in the house longer than she claimed she had. Long enough to go to her room and put her bag away. Perhaps even take her coat off. Then, after she discovered the body, she rushed back and put her coat on before giving the alarm, to make it look as though she'd just come in."

"Either that," I said, "or she got rid of the bag while she was out. Disposed of it, or stashed it away somewhere." I got up and went to the kitchen cupboard for more coffee.

"Making the question: What was she smuggling out of the house in that bag?"

The phone rang. Since he was nearest, Gerry answered it. I took a look at his face and went back to get more coffee for him, although he looked as though he needed something stronger.

"I see," he said noncommittally into the receiver. His expression grew progressively more thoughtful. I gathered he wished he had not picked up the phone; or, having done so, had taken the precaution of answering in a foreign accent, the better to maintain that it was Chang's Peking Laundry or Antonio's Flamenco Trattoria. I began to suspect that I knew who must be on the other end of the line.

"Yes, well, we'll see what we can do," he said, even less enthusiastically. "We can't promise anything, of course." He listened again in silence, then repeated, "We'll see what we can do," and cradled the receiver.

He sat there and looked at it glumly for a moment, then raised his head to demand of me, "Are we wife-minders?"

"Probably," I said. "What's the bad news?"

Gerry drew a long, shuddering breath. "That was Zayle on the line."

I nodded. I hadn't thought for a moment that it had been anyone else.

"Adele has left him, yet again," Gerry said. "He thinks she's heading back for those friends on the coast. *All*"—he was heavily ironic—"he wants us to do is nip across the street, patrol Charing Cross Station until she arrives, nab her, and escort her back home."

Well, we had faced more unreasonable requests from clients in our time. I sighed heavily.

"Do you think," Gerry asked, "it might help if we found new offices? Away from all Main Line stations?"

"That would be the signal"—I went to collect my coat—"for every client we possess to immediately want parcels picked up, friends met, children seen off to school, and any other damned thing you can think of, at every railway station in town. Just thank your stars that Adele's friends live in the right direction. We might have had to chase to Victoria or Euston."

"I don't see why we should have to do it." Gerry was still mutinous.

"Think of it this way," I said. "How would it look if the suspect's—our client's—wife walked out on him at this crucial stage? No one would exactly interpret it as a vote of confidence—least of all, the police. And when you think of the way it would look to the public, if the press got hold of it—as they would—"

"All right, you needn't labour the point." Gerry got up slowly. "But for God's sake, let's try to nab her before she gets us within pushing distance of any of those trains."

We caught up with her at the left luggage lockers. She didn't see us coming, being too occupied in searching through her handbag for the key which had obviously slipped to the bottom and lost itself in the litter of lipsticks, cosmetics, other keys, pens, loose coins, and all the other debris peculiar to the bottom of women's handbags.

We came up silently behind her and stood one on each side until she surfaced triumphantly with the key with the plastic numbered disc on the end. Then Gerry stepped forward.

"Allow me." He took the key from her hand and glanced at the number, looking to match it with the row of lockers.

She turned, as though to run, but I was blocking her on the other side.

"Here we are." He snapped open the locker and pulled out the case. I saw his eyebrows lift as he grunted in sudden surprise at the weight. "What do you have in here—the family silver?"

"You can take it back to him." Adele's immediate response betrayed that Gerry's guess had not been far off the mark. "But I'm not going back. Not even if you carry me!"

We met each other's eyes over her defiant head, mentally visualizing trying to carry a struggling redhead through Charing Cross Station. She'd probably scream, too—and I knew how penetrating that could be. We'd be lucky if we got off with a seven-to-ten-year sentence.

"Just as you please," Gerry said absently. His gaze roved to the noticeboards and I saw it linger on one advertising the Sealink Ferry to France from Folkestone. Even more absently, he hefted the case again, testing its weight. I knew his mind was busily following the same line as my own. Adele had packed valuables, rather than clothing. It was a coincidence that she had friends on the coast, but that was not where she had been intending to go.

Without taking her handbag away and checking it—a move she would resist as strongly as being removed from the station—we couldn't be sure, but I'd have bet she was carrying her passport. She could disappear on the Continent, selling off the valuables until she had found an alternative means of earning her keep—or until she judged it safe to return to England. Perhaps then she would go to her friends, but that was not her primary destination right now.

Had Zayle known that? Was that why he had sent us to find her and bring her back? Or had he wanted the return of whatever valuables she had packed in that case? More to the point, was he going to get what he wanted? So far as I was concerned, if it entailed a pitched battle with Adele the length of Charing Cross Station, she was as good as on that ferry right now.

I should have had more faith in Gerry. Just as Adele took a long, measuring look along the route to her train platform, as though considering her chances if she were to make a sudden break and sprint for the train at the last moment, Gerry sighed.

"I must say I admire you," he told the startled Adele. "I didn't know they made women like you anymore. Why, most women, finding out they were secretly engaged to a potential bigamist, would have just written him off and tried to keep the whole episode secret. But—"

"Bigamist?" Adele's eyes narrowed.

"But not you," Gerry continued firmly. "You loved him and you don't care who knows it. You're not sheltering behind your husband. You're going to stand up and be counted—with the other fiancées."

"Other fiancées?" A distinctly unpleasant note was creeping into Adele's echo. I decided to help the cause along.

"Hadn't you heard? The police have turned up two more—and that's just from the group in the surgery that afternoon. We don't know what the final score will be when they get around to checking out his outside, er, activities. And of course, the rest of his patients. He had quite a practice, hadn't he?"

The gate had swung open and the train to Folkestone was loading now, but Adele had lost interest. Her gaze was fixed somewhere on middle distance and her hands were clenching and unclenching at her sides. I had the impression that, if Tyler Meredith were not already dead, she would have killed him herself at this moment. Oddly enough, it cheered me. I felt she was the type to be more discreet about her emotions if she had really killed him.

"We mustn't keep you," Gerry said. "You don't want to miss your train."

I thought that was crowding our luck, but Adele gave no indication of having heard him. She seemed to be thinking deeply.

"We'll do our best," Gerry assured her, "to cover your tracks. From the press, I mean. But you must admit, it's a gift to them. 'Grieving Fiancée Number'—do you think they'll bill her Number One, Two, or Three?" He consulted me briefly before going on. "'Grieving Fiancée Flees Country. Deserted Husband Faces Fresh Police Grilling—'"

Adele's head snapped up proudly. "He did it for *me*," she declared.

"Who did what?" She had lost me.

"Endicott killed Tyler for my sake. To save me the humiliation of discovering what he was really like. I was blind not to see it before. Dear Endicott. I must go back immediately and tell him that I understand at last. That I'll forgive him and stand by him." She whirled about and started for the street exit.

That one left even Gerry gasping, and he had seen almost every variety of female rationalization.

He stared after her with a dumbfounded look. "You've got to stay single," he muttered, "it's the only protection."

"Come on." I picked up the case at his feet and gave him a shove. "She's getting away. We can't let her go back to Zayle without us. He'll think we haven't been on the job."

"The kindest thing we could do for Zayle," Gerry said grimly, "would be to shanghai Adele aboard that train and tell him we never found her."

I rather agreed, but it was too late. "She'd just get the next train back, now that she's changed her mind. I think we oversold her."

"I suppose there's no way to undo it?" The hopeless note in his voice betrayed that he already knew the answer. He had done his job too well.

"At least"—I tried to look on the bright side as we sprinted to catch up before she disappeared into the taxi she had hailed—"Zayle will be pleased."

"He probably will," Gerry said. "That man doesn't know when he's well off."

Adele didn't speak to us in the taxi and we were too out of breath to sustain much of a conversation, in any case. She had evidently ordered the driver to hurry, for he took corners and shortcuts with an enthusiasm which was more optimistic than realistic.

It didn't cheer me any to see a couple of familiar faces lurking outside the Zayle house as the taxi drew up. It was inevitable, of course. Two deaths in the same dentist's surgery were bound to attract a certain amount of journalistic interest. As Wilde once remarked, although not about patients: "To lose one . . . may be regarded as a misfortune; to lose both looks like carelessness." And who wants a careless dentist?

"Go straight up the steps," I told Adele. "Don't speak, don't answer any questions. Let us do the talking—if we have to."

She nodded and I hoped for the best. If she opened her mouth at all, it would be good for a two-column spread. If she gave the sort of statement she'd uttered to Gerry and me, it would make the front page. And where would our client be then? On his way to Wormwood Scrubs, thanks to his devoted wife.

"You've just been out shopping," Gerry briefed, obviously distrusting Adele's ability to keep silent as much as I did. "We saw you in the High Street on our way here and naturally stopped to pick you up."

Adele nodded again, still with a distant look. I took possession of the case, lest she reach for it from force of habit. Unfortunately, it didn't look much like a briefcase, but I was prepared to pull the "What elephant?" routine if anyone asked questions.

Gerry got out first and ran interference for Adele. She followed docilely, saying nothing, although I noticed she turned her head to the best angle as the photographers grabbed their shots.

I paid the driver and lingered to exchange a few harmless remarks with the press. Not even Royalty goes much on the "No comment" routine these days. There's nothing more guaranteed to enrage a reporter, and if you won't comment, *he* will. Or else he'll carefully print your "No comment" plus every question he asked leading up to it, leaving the readers to draw their own conclusions—which will be at least twice as libelous as anything he'd have dared to print.

They took it with fairly good grace, especially when I guaranteed to keep them posted, and I was timing my break for the moment Adele and Gerry got safely inside the house. I should have known things were going too smoothly.

We had reached one of those pauses in our question-and-answer game when the silence seemed to deepen and stretch out. I had just turned to move away when the front door at the top of the steps opened and General Sir Malcolm Zayle stood in the entrance. He ignored Gerry and gave Adele a cold look.

"So," he boomed out, "you decided to come back, did you?"

Chapter 11

"General! Sir! General!" I sprinted up the steps, pushing Adele and Gerry into the vestibule. The General fell back before our onslaught. " 'Careless talk,' General—" I reminded him, slamming the door in the faces of a couple of reporters who had bolted up the steps behind me.

" 'Costs lives,' " he finished. "Quite right. Quite right."

And the life it cost might be his son's. There was no point in elucidating, however. I leaned weakly against the door and tried to pretend no one was hammering indignantly at it.

"Quite right," the General said again. He frowned at the door. "Is that The Enemy out there?"

"It depends on how you look at it," I told him. "They're the press."

"Don't like the press." His reaction was instantaneous. "Never get anything right. Always misquoting."

"Never mind," I said as the hammering tapered off, "we don't have to open the door."

"Quite right. Let them stay out there." He snorted. "Pity it isn't snowing."

There were a few halfhearted yodels through the letter flap and then quiet. We had a moment of silence all round, then Sir Malcolm stepped forward briskly.

"Let me take your case, m'dear, and show you to your room."

I relinquished Adele's case to him, wondering who he thought she was this time. She didn't appear to know, either. She gave him a noncommittal smile, suitable for an errant daughter-in-law, shy houseguest, or new parlourmaid, and followed him up the stairs.

There had seemed to be no indication that we should trail along, so Gerry and I stayed where we were, tacitly debating, with lifts of eyebrows, tilts of heads, and twitching of shoulders, whether or not we should deploy ourselves in the waiting room.

The question was settled for us when Penny appeared at the head of the stairs and motioned for us to come up—quietly. We took the stairs in a tiptoe rush and she led us into Zayle's surgery and closed the door.

"I think you ought to see Mr. Zayle," she said earnestly. "I really think you ought to."

Gerry and I looked at each other, then glanced around the surgery. Zayle wasn't there. Presumably, he'd gone upstairs to greet his returning wife.

"What do you mean?" Gerry asked.

At the same moment, I said defensively, "I'm perfectly all right. Did he put you up to this?" That idée fixe of his about my troublesome tooth was becoming a damned nuisance.

"I just think you ought to see him," she said to both of us impartially. "That's all. Before anyone else does, I mean."

"What's the matter?" Gerry asked. "Who else is supposed to see him this morning?"

"If she can get away from her photography session in time, Morgana Fane is coming. He hasn't been able to fit her in yet, and I think she's getting annoyed about it."

And who could blame her? Her time was worth considerably more than a society dentist's. Not to mention the fact that she had considerably less of it in which to gather rosebuds and sitting fees. A few wrinkles wouldn't deter Zayle's clientele, but Morgana Fane's opportunities to increase her fortune would not continue forever. It was lucky for her that she was marrying well, but some models still like to keep going as long as they're in demand.

"Isn't she super?" Penny sighed. "We had her X rays out yesterday. Would you believe it, she has *four* capped teeth? Right in front, too. You'd never know it, would you?"

"That's the whole idea with caps," I said, but

Penny wasn't paying attention. Her gaze turned to a glossy magazine, open on the desk, with which she had obviously been whiling away Zayle's absence. Morgana Fane in full colour sprawled across a double-page spread in some crazed designer's fantasy of what the well-undressed prostitute would wear this year.

"All her clothes look so lovely on her," Penny said wistfully. "I wish clothes would look like that on *me*."

"Just remember"—something was niggling at me, but Penny's misplaced values were niggling more—"she only has to worry about how she looks from the front. You don't see the back view.

"In fact"—I warmed to my subject—"it would be highly salutary if all fashion-mad females could see the reverse side of these high-fashion photos. You, too, could achieve perfection in any modest little ten-pound-ninety-five-pence number if you had six safety pins, two clothes pegs, and the photographer's assistant clinging on for dear life behind."

"I suppose so." Penny relinquished her dream reluctantly. "Anyway, I can get a super medallion like hers. *That* isn't a photographic trick."

"No," I agreed, "but if you do get one, just don't wear it to work. I couldn't stand looking at it for longer than ten seconds a day—"

"Ah, there you are, there you are!" Zayle bustled into the surgery. "You're lucky, very lucky. I've had an unexpected cancellation. That means I can take you now."

He was looking straight at me.

"I'm all right." I backed away. "There's nothing wrong with any of my teeth. They're all fine."

"That's what they all say." He shook his head at me in exasperation. "And then they telephone me at two A.M. with a raging toothache and expect me to do something about it there and then."

It was manifestly unfair. I'd never telephoned him outside of office hours during our entire association—which was more than he could say about his treatment of Perkins & Tate.

"Penny"—he continued to treat us in his accustomed style—"go upstairs and see if Mrs. Zayle would like a cup of tea or anything else—and get it for her if she does." Penny left the room.

"And"—he turned to Gerry—"we won't need you for this. You can wait downstairs." Before I could stop him, Gerry had gone, too.

"Now"—Zayle gave me an oily smile—"if you'll just sit down in the chair and make yourself comfortable . . ."

He had to be joking. I stared at him blankly, wondering if there was any way of getting to him through this obsession he had developed about my teeth. Then I looked again, more closely. There was something odd about Endicott Zayle—odder than usual, I mean. Possibly it was the white surgeon's cap perched on the top of his head. It was undoubtedly very hygienic, but it gave him an eccentric appearance.

"Sit down!" There was a fractious note in his voice. "What's the matter—don't you like my chair?"

"No," I said truthfully.

His face crumpled, but if he didn't want to hear

the answers, he shouldn't ask the questions. "Why don't people like my chair?" He sniffed. "Why don't people like me?" His eyes were shining suspiciously.

"Now, now," I placated, backing a bit farther. "I'm sure they do."

"They don't. Everybody hates us." He snuffled unpleasantly again. I began to wonder if he'd had a scene with Adele. She might have done another about-face on the subject of returning to him. Something had certainly upset him.

"No, no, I'm sure—"

"Don't try to fool me—I *know*. We *all* know," he added darkly.

"You do?" I got a bit more distance between us. Not that it did much good. He advanced as I retreated. "*All* of you, eh?" I wondered if it could still be called schizophrenia when the subject thought he was several people.

"Dentists and psychiatrists," he said. "We have the highest suicide rates of any of the professions. And do you know why?"

"Because everybody hates you?" It slipped out automatically. I closed my mouth and tried to look as though it hadn't come from me.

"That's right," he said. "You admit it. You see— everyone knows."

"I'm sure you're exaggerating," I said. "Someone must love you." Immediately, I wished I hadn't brought that up. If he followed though on it, I was going to have to admit I couldn't name one person. His father was off in some remote world of his own; his partner had been betraying him; his wife had planned to elope with his partner; the cards all seemed stacked against him.

"It isn't fair," he said, and even though I'd been thinking that myself, I began to lose sympathy. "It's the ingratitude of everyone that hurts. Dentists and psychiatrists—who else makes you so comfortable? Who works so hard for you?"

"You mustn't brood," I said. "All professions have their ups and downs. If you think public relations work is easy—"

"It's the ingratitude," he said again, obviously having no time for anyone's problems other than his own. Unless they were a psychiatrist, that is.

"Think of it. We provide you with a nice comfortable chair, a cozy couch—and you lie back and hate us. No wonder the suicide rate is so high. We do everything we can for you, and all the time you're lying there comfortably, we know that down deep you're hating us."

"I wouldn't say that," I said. Personally, I was working up quite a good loathing of him from a vertical position. It had never occurred to me before, but if there was one thing I hated more than a dentist, it was a maudlin dentist.

"You wouldn't?" He looked unexpectedly hopeful and I was glad he couldn't read my mind.

"Not at all." I didn't consider it a lie—it was just good PR to keep up your client's morale.

"Then"—he looked at me suspiciously—"why won't you get in my chair?"

"Actually," I improvised, "I think I have a cold coming on. My throat feels raw and scratchy. You don't want to examine me in this condition. I might spread germs all over the place."

"You talk as though dentistry were still in the nineteenth century." He seemed to take it personally. "We sterilize everything before we use it on anyone else." As though to punctuate his remarks, he stabbed at the steam cabinet and the top flew open with a slight hiss, displaying rows of shining instruments. To my nervous eyes, there seemed to be a faint cloud of steam rising all around them.

"But you—" I said quickly. "You don't want to catch my cold. It would be terrible for you. And I'd feel so guilty—"

"You needn't worry about that," he said quite cheerfully. He turned and pulled something from a drawer. "Now then"—he turned back, a gauze surgical mask covering his nose and chin—"you can't do me any harm. Just get into that chair and we'll take a look at what's troubling you."

He could do that by looking in a mirror. The surgical mask did nothing to reassure me; it gave him a sinister, dehumanized appearance. The beady little eyes glaring at me over the top seemed to be loosing what patience they had.

"Come, come," he said, "get into the chair. We don't have all day, you know. Other patients will be arriving for their appointments."

It was a hopeful thought, but the door remained firmly closed. Where was Penny? Where was Gerry? Why had they deserted me like this? I took another step backward and stumbled over something. It was the step of the chair.

"That's right. Upsy-daisy." He caught my arm and hurled me into the chair.

"Well." Since I no longer seemed to have a choice, I capitulated, but I was going down fighting. "Just a checkup, remember? Just my six-monthly checkup. Ha-ha. I'm a bit overdue for it, I'm afraid."

"Mmm-hmm." He whipped a white bib around my neck and tied it with unnecessary vigour. "You needn't be afraid. We'll find the tooth that's bothering you. Open wide. . . ."

"Now look—" I said. "*Yeee-ow!*"

"Aha." He surfaced triumphantly, waving the needle-pointed probe. "I knew we'd find it." The tip of the probe was dulled with red—*my* blood.

"You never got anywhere near a tooth," I protested. "You jabbed that thing into my gum."

"That's just your imagination," he soothed. "It just felt to you as though I did."

"You did," I said stubbornly.

"No—no. All in your mind. It's all psychological, you know. Dentistry and psychiatry are closely allied. That's why people are so deeply afraid of the dentist. They fear having a tooth pulled. It's a manifestation of the castration complex. And women can have it, too, you know."

"Umm," I said. I thought of riposting with the other popular theory: that people become dentists, surgeons, etc., as a means of sublimating their sadistic tendencies. On second thought, I decided not to go into that right now. Like the dying Irishman who refused to renounce the Devil and all his works, I felt "I'm not in a position to antagonize anyone at a time like this."

"Oh, it's very common you know. Very common. You'd be surprised—"

"Ummm," I said again. The thought of a psychological discussion with Zayle held no allure for me. I tried to look as though I'd never heard of Jung or Adler. And if he dragged Freud into it, I'd say I'd gone off him since his last recipe exploded in the oven.

"Now, then . . ." He'd been fiddling with something just beyond my range of vision, and now he moved back into view. He still held the probe in one hand. With the other, he was pulling forward the drilling equipment.

"Now . . ." He leaned into my mouth again. "Let me get a fix on that tooth and we'll . . ."

I pressed back into the chair, trying to burrow my way out through the back as he put a hand that seemed to have at least twelve fingers into my mouth and followed it with that deadly sharp probe again.

I fought for breath and suddenly I got too much of it. His breath. Through the surgical mask and all. I told myself it couldn't be true and sniffed wildly. There was no doubt about it.

A lot of things which had been confusing me about this whole situation became clear. No wonder the conversation was so odd, his fixation on my tooth so pronounced. In his condition, it was scarcely surprising that he had forgotten my agonizing molar was just a cover story we had cooked up between us.

Our eminent Harley Street dental surgeon was drunk as a skunk.

"I see it!" he crowed. "Now, just stay right

there—" He pulled the drill down into position and prepared to move in.

"Wait a minute!" I protested wildly. "Wait a minute—can't we talk this over?"

"Talk?" He drew back slightly. "Talk what over?"

I was in no mood for social niceties. "You've been drinking!" I accused.

"Drinking?" He drew himself up huffily, and now that I was concentrating on him rather than on his waiting instruments, I could notice a distinct sway.

"Drinking!"

"Are you suggesting"—he squinted down at me, seeming to have some difficulty in focusing— "simply because I may have had a drink or two to brace myself while I waited for my dear wife to be restored to me, that I'm *incapable*?"

"I didn't say that." Furtively, I braced my feet against the footrest of the chair and gripped the arms, trying to lever myself into a more upright position. I was at a distinct disadvantage with him looming over me like that.

"You *meant* it." His sense of grievance, never very far away, was rising to the fore again. "I'll have you know I'm a *dentist*! I—" It did not reassure me that, at this point, he attempted to strike his chest and missed, delivering a glancing blow to his left shoulder. "I could do this job blindfolded!"

In the circles I move in, I've heard artists and writers declare they can work as well drunk as they can sober, and it never occurred to me to dispute them. It didn't seem to matter all that much. The worst that could happen would be that they'd whack hell out of a piece of canvas or a few sheets of paper, and in the cold, gray light of morning, they could chuck the whole thing away if the results didn't please them.

But this was *my* mouth Zayle was proposing to head into with a supersonic drill. I edged forward in the chair, preparing to bolt.

"Why don't we go and have a cup of coffee?" I suggested cagily, realizing as I did so that this was why Penny hadn't come back. She wasn't to know that we had got our signals crossed.

I knew now what she had meant when she had insisted that one of us ought to "see" Zayle—"see to him," she should have said. And she was tactfully staying out of the way, imagining that this was what I was doing. By this time, she was trustingly supposing me to have poured several cups of black coffee down his gullet, and perhaps even have shoved his head under a cold-water tap—or into his spittoon.

I immediately wished I hadn't thought of that.

"I'm dying for a cup of coffee." And that wasn't a happy phrasing, either. I struggled forward in the chair, my feet seeking the floor.

"That tooth needs taking care of!" He did something sneaky with the foot pedal and the chair tilted backward throwing me onto a horizontal plane. Zayle loomed over me, a white-masked face swimming above my eyes. "Plenty of time for coffee later."

Coffee for one? It sounded too much like it. I wriggled over to one side of the chair. I had never liked the dentist's office, but until recently I had never been so painfully aware of all the death traps lurking in it. The anaesthetic, the spittoon—even those rolls of cotton which had been used to plug the waste pipe could just as easily have been rammed down an open throat. The potentialities of the probes didn't bear thinking about—nor did that drill being pulled down into position. Three thousand revolutions per minute, being aimed at my back molar by that unsteady hand. His squinting eyes made me suspect he might be seeing two of me, and God knew how many molars.

"Stay still, damn you," he muttered. "How can I work with you twisting around like an eel?" I heard the motor rev up as he fitted a burred drill head into the holder and checked to see that it was secure.

It was a time for desperate measures, and as his stubby fingers probed into my mouth just ahead of the drill, I took them. My teeth clamped over those fingers—if he couldn't get them out, he couldn't get the drill in.

As it happened, he nearly dropped the drill. His scream, I was surprised to note, was nearly as soprano as his wife's. "You bit me!" He wrenched his fingers away. "You *bit* me!"

"Sorry about that," I said feebly. "Reflex action, you know." He didn't look as though he believed me.

"You deliberately bit me!" he said. You'd think a dentist would be used to that sort of thing, but it seemed to be preying on his mind. "You hate me!"

"No, no." Smiling ingratiatingly, I tried to get out of the chair while he was still brooding.

I didn't make it. He did something with his foot again and the chair tilted and swerved as though it had some diabolic life of its own. They were both in league against me.

"Well, let me tell you." He slammed me against the back of the chair with the flat of one hand. The other hand held a madly whirring drill. "I hate you lousy rotten patients, too!"

As he moved in, I was torn between closing my eyes and hoping the Lord that looked after fools, children, and drunkards would fit me in somewhere amongst them, or keeping my eyes wide open and fighting to the last ditch.

Neither of us heard the surgery door open.

"Oh, sorry." Inspector Rennolds stood in the doorway. "I wanted to speak to you. I didn't realize you were busy. I'll come back later—"

Chapter 12

"Eh?" Zayle turned away to peer muzzily at the figure hovering in the doorway.

"No, no." While his attention was distracted, I lunged from the chair. "I'll come now. Always glad to do my duty as a citizen." He hadn't said which of us he wanted to speak to, so I was going to claim the honour before Zayle could.

"Besides, I have something to tell you." I made the doorway in a standing broad jump and grabbing his arm, whirled him about and gained the safety of the corridor. "Vital information to impart,"

I babbled. "Delay might be fatal. Let's have a talk right now."

He was still gazing over his shoulder at Zayle in a puzzled way as I dragged him up the stairs. As I shut the living room door, I saw that he was now looking at me with the same puzzled gaze. There was suspicion in his look, as well, for which I couldn't blame him. I had never voluntarily sought an interview with him before. I doubt if many people had.

"Well." I let go of his arm and gave him a placating smile. "This is better." I suspected that was even more of a lie than I intended. It was better than the dental chair, but it was beginning to feel like out of the frying pan into the fire.

"What"—I took the initiative—"did you want to see me about?"

"I didn't." His steady gaze was unnerving. "I wanted to talk to the dentist."

"Oh, well, in that case—" I started for the door. "I'll clear out of your way and let you get on with it." I almost made it. I had my hand on the doorknob when his hand fell on my shoulder and turned me back.

"You said you had something to tell me," he reminded me. " 'Vital information to impart.' "

"Oh, that." I winced at the direct quotation. "On second thought—"

"Why don't we sit down and talk it over." He moved me inexorably away from the door. "Perhaps you'll have a third thought."

I couldn't say he actually pushed, but I found myself floundering on the sofa while he took the straight chair opposite. "All right," he said, "begin."

Begin. I rummaged wildly through my store-cupboard of guilty knowledge—which was uncomfortably crowded—for some fairly innocuous piece of information I could toss to him. There wasn't much. I decided to opt for the obvious and give him something he might already have noticed for himself.

"Endicott Zayle," I said. "I thought I ought to talk to you about him. I mean, I've known him for some time, and you've never seen him before?" I waited for his affirmative nod, then continued, "There's something wrong about him lately. Odd, I mean. He hasn't been himself. He keeps getting these strange ideas and can't be talked out of them—" I stopped. Rennolds had leaned back, a pained expression on his face.

"I see," he said. "So that's it. You're working up to a 'detained at the Queen's pleasure.' I might have known it."

He stopped me cold with that one. After a moment, I got my mouth closed again, but still couldn't think of anything to say. I needn't have bothered. He was in full spate and quite bitter about it all.

"You're planning to bring in the psychiatrists to prove it all goes back to an unhappy childhood; then you'll get the trendies, who'll moan about cruel treatment and police brutality. And then there'll be the bleeding hearts, who think he ought to be given a medal because he only knocked off a couple of people who irritated him instead of running amok down Regent Street with a machine gun during rush hour. After that, you'll parade the do-gooders to claim—"

"He didn't do it." I found my voice at last. "My client is innocent."

That stopped *him* cold. "All the indications point to Endicott Zayle," he said almost irritably.

"He didn't do it." Even to my own ears, my voice sounded firm and convincing. It almost stilled the little quiver of doubt deep within me. Almost.

"You think so?" He stared at me reflectively for a moment, then moved suddenly. I didn't know what was coming, but tried not to flinch. He reached out and snatched the forgotten white bib from around my neck and tossed it onto the coffee table between us. "That's been distracting me," he said in not quite apology.

"I'd forgotten it," I admitted, glancing at it where it lay on top of a pile of papers he had obviously been working on, partially obscuring them. Or was that the idea? Was there something there he didn't want me to see? But it looked innocent enough—what I could see of it—largely magazines, what looked like a couple of theatre programmes, and—probably the real meat—a small sheaf of nondescript carbon flimsies. I wondered what he'd do if I were to pick up the bib and fold it neatly, replacing it on the table beside the pile of papers, so that I could read the top ones.

"Can you prove it?" he demanded, startling me out of any further plans for prying.

"Prove what?"

"That he's innocent?" It was like a gauntlet flung down before me. I wondered whether he was challenging me to work against him. If so, I didn't want to know.

"That's your job," I said hastily. "I have enough to do in my own. PR keeps me busy enough without taking on amateur sleuthing as well."

"Good." He settled back in his chair. "You just hold on to that attitude." He seemed mollified, and although I couldn't say he was exactly friendly, he seemed at least to have shifted into neutral toward me. It was a big improvement.

"We *are* working, you know." He was almost chatty. "You—the public—never realize how much background work goes on. We're working, always working, digging into the pasts of everyone involved in a case. *That's* where you get most of your real information—and your motives."

He paused; his mouth twisted oddly, smoothed out, and twisted again. I lost the slight sense of comfort I had had. Was he making faces at me? Was I supposed to gather something from those expressions? If I was, I needed more time to work on it. We'd never been on the same wavelength and this wasn't helping matters.

"I'm sure you're right," I said, and watched his mouth contort again. It was beginning to hold a hypnotic fascination for me. What did he imagine he was conveying? Was there someone listening at the door, so that he was telling me one thing while warning me to pay no attention to whatever he said? But he hadn't said anything pertinent.

"That's where most cases are solved—in the past," he emphasized. His cheek bulged briefly and returned to normal. "Inquiries are proceeding—you may be sure of that. Now"—he changed tone so abruptly that I was further unnerved—"was there something else you wanted to tell me?"

"No, no," I disclaimed hastily. "I'm sure I couldn't tell you a thing you don't already know. You're doing a great job. Just keep it up and—"

I was afraid I was overdoing it. His mouth seemed to try to tie itself into a knot. I closed my eyes, and when I opened them again, he was still staring at me suspiciously.

"All right." I decided to be honest and throw myself on his mercy—if any. "It was all a load of old codswallop. I don't have anything to tell. I just wanted to get out of that chair before Zayle started drilling."

"Why? What's the matter?" His voice rose on a note of panic. "Isn't he a good dentist?"

"One of the best," I assured him quickly. His reaction had suddenly given me the key to the situation. All those faces and mouths twistings were the result of a man probing a tender tooth with his tongue. No wonder he'd wanted to speak to the dentist, he'd probably been trying to arrange an appointment.

"Endicott Zayle," I said firmly, "is one of the top dentists in London. *And* he takes a few patients on the National Health. I'm one, and Gerry is another. We have every confidence in him."

"Ummm," the inspector said dubiously. Our recommendation didn't carry much weight with him.

"How long has it been bothering you?" I asked. This was better, bringing an immediate response. Talking about dental troubles with people who have

them is nearly as satisfying as discussing the finer
points of surgery with a postoperative case.

"Two or three days. It started with just a niggling ache and I thought it would go away." I'd
never heard him so forthcoming before. "Then it
got worse and worse and aspirin doesn't help anymore. I think the stopping's going to fall out. It's
loose. It wobbles when I touch it." He demonstrated
with his tongue and winced again.

"Yes, yes," I said quickly before he opened his
mouth and invited me to look inside. That was usually the next step and I'd sooner leave it to Zayle—
that was the sort of thing *he* got paid for doing.

"Come with me." I stood up. "We'll go and see
Endicott Zayle right now." Then I remembered the
condition Zayle was in. "Er—perhaps we ought to
speak to the receptionist first."

But he was halfway to the door. That tooth must
really be bothering him. I'd never seen anyone so
eager to leap into a dentist's chair.

Then he faltered and I thought a normal reaction
was setting in at last. "Wait a minute," he said. "I
can't have it attended to now. I have to get over to
the House."

For a moment I wondered whether some sudden
emergency had arisen at home requiring his presence, then I realized what he meant.

"Make her give you tea on the terrace," I said.
"It's a nice afternoon for it." We were in the downstairs hallway now and he was looking around inde-
cisively, as though he might still prefer the dentist to
the call of duty. He wouldn't if he got a good look at
the dentist right now—a thing I had to prevent. I

ought also to check on how many patients were in the waiting room and have a quiet word with the receptionist before hunting out a source of black coffee and making sure Zayle drank enough of it to do him some good. It's one of the more depressing aspects of public relations—the amount of time we have to spend simply trying to protect the client from himself.

"*If* you'll pardon me . . . " We were blocking the top of the stairs and Morgana Fane was trying to edge past us. Behind her, Penny was signaling to me with a worried look on her face. Gerry, looking even more worried, brought up the rear—I could see that Penny had explained the situation to him with more clarity than she had explained it to me.

"Oops, sorry." I managed to block Morgana's way still further, while shaking my head to Penny and Gerry. "Sorry again." We went into one of those sidestepping encounters in which I kept blocking her way every time she tried to pass. They usually happen only by accident and it took some pretty tricky footwork on my part to keep blocking her; she was a lot more nimble-footed than I was.

"Get Adele!" I mouthed to Penny over Morgana's head. Penny nodded and slipped past us as we waltzed over to the left.

"Now see here." Morgana stopped abruptly and faced me, eyes glittering as dangerously as her medallion. "I have only half an hour before my next session. I *must* see my dentist now—without wasting any time. He promised to fit me in."

It would take more than half an hour to sober him up. I took a deep breath and reminded myself that what I was doing was for her own good, as well as our client's.

"Terribly sorry," I said. "In fact, he intended to fit you in, but he miscalculated. Rather, there was a sudden emergency and he couldn't reach you in time to put you off. He's closeted with the emergency right now."

Behind me, I was aware that Inspector Rennolds stirred restlessly, as though he might be going to say something contradictory. I stepped backward sharply and felt my heel come down on his toe.

"Sorry," I apologized over my shoulder. Ignoring his snort of outrage, I shifted position to block Morgana as she tried advancing again.

It was an impasse and we had another brief waltz, during which her temper didn't improve. I was feeling a bit fraught myself.

"There you are," a voice thundered behind me. Those of us not facing that way swiveled about to see General Sir Malcolm bearing down on us.

"Yes, sir." Determined to keep in good with at least one figure of authority, I saluted. But he paid no attention to me.

"I have something for you," he continued. Gerry flinched and sidled away, but he wasn't the target this time.

"Here!" From behind his back, General Sir Malcolm brought out a long white plume and presented it to Inspector Rennolds. "Think it over well," he said sternly. "It's not too late."

"Er, thank you." Rennolds took the feather with a slightly dazed expression.

"Now ..." Business out of the way, General Sir

Malcolm transferred his attention to Morgana. "Who is going to introduce me to this delightful little lady?" he said, beaming.

I was surprised to see Morgana turn pale. Perhaps she hadn't realized the slipperiness of the General's faulty grasp on reality. More likely, she wasn't accustomed to anyone's forgetting they'd met her before—no matter what condition they were in.

"Grandmother's fan!" Adele's anguished wail focused our attention on her as she descended the stairs. "General—you promised!"

"Well," Gerry muttered, "at least we know one thing she had packed in that suitcase."

"Father?" The surgery door opened. "Is that you?" Endicott Zayle peered out nervously. "Father, I want to speak to you."

"Bah!" General Sir Malcolm whirled on his heel in an abrupt about-face, nearly colliding with Adele, who had come up behind him.

"General—" She turned and followed him.

"Father—wait—" Endicott Zayle came out of the surgery, not too obviously unsteady, I was relieved to note, and went after the others.

Penny flattened herself against the wall as they all swept up the staircase past her. Just one big happy family. Looking a bit shaken, Penny then continued down the stairs to join us in the hallway.

"It's all right," I said. "Adele can take care of it now."

There was a sigh of defeat from Morgana—she wasn't going to be able to squeeze any treatment into *this* spare half hour. Although—

"I must go." She looked at her watch. "I have a

photo session in Bond Street. Perhaps I can get a cab—"

"Let me drop you." Rennolds came back to life. "It's on my way."

I wouldn't have said that, but it wasn't all that much of a detour, either. And he had a police car at his disposal.

"How kind of you." Morgana gave him an automatic smile.

"Not at all." His eyes followed her trim trouser-suited figure down the stairs, then turned back to us. He seemed to notice the white feather still in his hand and was momentarily bemused again.

"That's right." Gerry slapped him on the back. "'We Don't Want to Lose You, but We Think You Ought to Go.'"

"I'll give that back to Adele." I took the feather from his hand. "She'll be getting the fan restored again. And"—I forestalled his nervous comment—"I'll make an appointment for you with Endicott."

"After work, if possible," he said. "If it wouldn't be too much trouble."

"About seven," I said. "And it won't be any trouble at all." Frankly, I hoped it would ruin Zayle's evening. I felt he had it coming—look at the way he'd disrupted Perkins & Tate.

"Fine." He looked as though he might be going to say more, but Morgana Fane was waiting impatiently at the foot of the stairs. "Fine," he said again, and exited.

"Everything seems to be under control here," Gerry said. "Do you think we might spare a few minutes for the office now?"

"We'd better, if we plan to keep the business running." I handed the white plume to Penny. "Give this to one of the Zayles—not the General, for God's sake—when you see them and—"

"Shan't I come with you?" she asked. "Work must be piling up dreadfully back there."

"Thanks." I resisted the impulse to take advantage of her good nature; she'd been working hard here. "You hold down the fort here until Zayle's nurse recovers. We'll try to manage as best we can without you."

"Come *on*," Gerry said, "before something else happens."

Chapter 13

We returned to pandemonium. The telephone was ringing insistently and the cat was howling with fury. I caught up one with each hand, but Pandora twisted free and I had to let her drop back on the desktop. I ought to have dropped the telephone.

It was one of our paying clients—he didn't pay much, but he paid—inquiring truculently why we hadn't mounted a major publicity campaign to inform the world that he could currently be seen in a new film. (In which he appeared for all of five minutes—two of them consecutive—and uttered six lines.) He had, he added, been trying to reach us for several days, but no one ever answered the phone—perhaps we were in the process of retiring?

The client was more easily placated than the cat. Perjury cut no ice with Pandora. She stamped up and down the desk, letting us have it in no uncertain terms.

"It sounds like an ultimatum," Gerry said.

"Her meals *have* been fairly irregular for the past couple of days." I could see her side of it; it was a pity we couldn't explain ours to her. Not that she was in any mood to listen. She leaped to the floor and vented a bit more spleen by sharpening her claws on one leg of the desk, muttering to herself.

"We ought to get her a scratching post when finances run to it," Gerry said, looking at the splintered leg. "At this rate, it won't take long to saw through that leg completely."

"There are three more," I said callously, heading for the emergency rations. We kept a store of cat food, but there were also tins of kippers and sardines tucked away for peacemaking or rewards. Although Pandora ate cat food happily enough, she really preferred people food.

Pandora abandoned the desk and came after me, scolding. I needn't think I was going to get round her that way.

Her milk saucer was empty, too. I hurriedly splashed some milk into it to decoy her while I got the tin open. Otherwise, she had a nasty habit of trying to get between the tin opener and the tin, presumably on some theory that she was helping me to open it faster. It was a good way to lose a set of whiskers.

Kippers turfed into the again-empty milk saucer, I put on the kettle for coffee. We'd had the forethought to stop and pick up pork pies along the way, so dinner wouldn't take long. More important, we could eat it while we worked.

I had poured the coffee and was sitting down to the typewriter when I noticed Pandora looking at me reflectively. She had finished her kippers and had washed her face. Now what she wanted was a lap to settle down in for a nap.

"Friends?" I suggested.

It wasn't going to be quite that easy. She gave me an outraged glare and started toward Gerry. Then she wavered, obviously remembering that he was no better than I was. We had both gone away and left her. She stood there, hesitating.

"Friends?" I tried again.

She considered it carefully, her concentration broken by a wide yawn.

"Come on." I patted my lap invitingly. "Be friends."

"Prryeh!" Abruptly she abandoned the vendetta and dived for my lap.

"That's better." She settled down, I went back to writing press releases, and Gerry manned the telephone.

After a couple of hours, we switched over. Gerry worked on press releases and I took the telephone, contacting neglected clients and trying to make them feel less neglected, while not actually tying us down to doing anything like seeing them.

Then Gerry put the kettle on again and we stopped for a breather and a cup of coffee. Pandora accepted a saucer of milk, chirruping under her breath that this was more like it. A nice quiet evening at home, with two laps available and refreshment at frequent intervals. We were all feeling pleasantly relaxed and virtuous about getting some work done at last. We should have known it couldn't last.

The telephone rang.

Being nearest, I answered it—an unfortunate habit I've never been able to break.

"Hello?" The voice was low, cautious, guarded—but I recognized it immediately.

"Penny! What's the matter?"

She did not question my assuming something was the matter—which was the most telling sign of all.

"I—I don't know. It's just—I don't know. Perhaps it's because I'm alone here and—"

"Alone? Where are the others?"

"Upstairs in the flat. And I—I just suddenly wanted to talk to someone. I'm all right, really. It's silly, I know."

It wasn't silly. Not in that house.

"Penny, listen. If anything's upset you—anything at all—you walk straight out of that house and come here. Take a taxi—we'll pay at this end."

"No, really, nothing's happened. I'm feeling better already and Mr. Zayle needs me here. He still has more appointments. We're working late tonight."

And it was my fault. Hoping to inconvenience Zayle, I'd unwittingly put Penny on the spot. That made me feel great.

"Penny," I tried again, "Penny, forget all that. Put down the phone and walk straight out and get into a cab. Don't even wait to collect your coat. Come back here—"

"I'm sorry, sir." Penny's voice became cool and professional. "I must go now. A patient has just come in."

"Penny—" But she had rung off.

I put down the phone. "I don't like it."

"Neither do I." Gerry was reaching for his coat. "Let's get over there."

"Nrryoh!" The only dissenting vote was Pandora's. Sensing desertion again, she streaked across the room, leaped to the desktop and from there to my shoulder, where she crouched, digging in her claws.

"Pandora, get down!" I slanted my shoulders, trying to tilt her back onto the desk. She gripped harder with her claws and cursed me soundly.

"Let her come," Gerry said. "We don't have time to fool around." He, too, felt a sense of urgency.

"You won't like it," I warned her. She hitched herself closer around my neck—I wasn't going to get rid of her that way.

"Come *on*!" Gerry said.

The street was deserted when our taxi rolled up in front of Zayle, Zayle & Meredith. Not even a reporter lurking anywhere nearby. Nor a policeman. Evidently the story had cooled down. It wasn't important enough anymore to keep anyone on overtime. The thought ought to have cheered me, but it didn't.

"I don't like it," Gerry said as we paid off the cab and crossed the pavement. "I just don't like it."

Neither did Pandora. She began a deep subvocal rumbling when the smell of antiseptic in the front hall reached her nostrils.

"You *would* come," I reminded her. "It was your own idea."

She shifted uneasily on my shoulder and snarled softly. She flexed her claws in the cloth of my coat, obviously preparing to fight to the end.

The reception desk was empty; our footsteps echoed back at us in the waiting room. Gerry and I exchanged an unhappy look.

"I don't know about you," Gerry said, "but I feel like the first man aboard the *Mary Celeste*—afterwards."

I nodded glumly, wishing he hadn't bothered to verbalize the situation. A thought like that was all I needed.

"There *must* be someone around." Gerry turned and made for the hallway again with me behind him. "Penny was here just a few minutes ago."

"A patient came in," I recalled. "She's probably upstairs in the surgery, passing the probes and handing swabs to Zayle."

"It's awfully quiet up there." Gerry cast a worried glance up the stairs.

"There isn't usually much noise, anyway." The implication that the surgery must be empty because no one was screaming up there was disquieting, but Gerry seemed to have settled in for a steady run of gloom. I wished fleetingly that I had tried to persuade him to remain at the office and telephone a few more clients. On the other hand, I was just as glad not to be alone in this house at the moment.

"Let's go up—" I began, when another voice cut across mine.

"Attention!"

Automatically, I snapped to attention, noting out of the corner of my eye that Gerry had done the same. Pandora rocked on my shoulder, complaining at being jounced about so.

General Sir Malcolm descended the stairs, obviously bent on inspecting the troops. This comparative normalcy cheered me. Things might not be so bad as we feared if General Sir Malcolm were carrying on in his usual way. Even he had noticed it when there had been a couple of corpses around the place. Perhaps we'd just been letting our nerves get the better of us.

"I'm looking for Geoffrey," he announced. He glared at me. "You're his adjutant. Where is he? He was due here half an hour ago."

"Emergency conference, sir," I improvised quickly. "Called without warning. He sent me along to tell you he'd be here as soon as he could." The General seemed to be in a martial mood, and after all, Sir Geoffrey had stepped in originally and saved me a lot of bother. The least I could do was repay in kind. At the same time, I wondered whether the appointment had been for tonight or for some distant night in a decade long past.

"I see." The General frowned. "Right," he ordered. "Come upstairs."

We'd been heading in that direction, anyway.

General Sir Malcolm looked back over his shoulder several times. Pandora's presence seemed to

bother him—a Siamese cat was not regulation issue.
True, I was still in mufti until my uniform arrived,
but even so—

On the other hand, I remembered that Pandora
had seemed to upset Endicott Zayle in some myste-
rious way. Perhaps the whole Zayle family had a
thing about Siamese cats.

"Come in." The General swung open the door to
the living quarters on the second floor. It was evident
that he seldom entertained in his own small flat.
We followed him inside.

"Sit down." The invitation still had the ring of a
command. We sat.

The smell of disinfectant was not evident in
here. Pandora felt reassured enough to leave my
shoulder and slither into my lap, although she kept a
wary eye on the door. If it opened, she was prepared to fly for her life.

The General had remained standing. Now he
began to pace the room. He knew we were there, but
I wondered if he knew who we were. There was no
particular recognition in the sharp glances he slanted
at us as he paced past.

"I must ask you to keep what I am about to
tell you in strictest confidence," he warned us, evidently coming to some decision and sitting down in
the chair opposite us. Even Pandora stirred uneasily
at that; the knowledge that it boded no good was in
the air.

"There has been a strange woman lurking about
headquarters recently," he continued. "Behaving in
an odd manner. I'll be candid—I suspect espionage."

"You see," Gerry muttered, "I knew we'd get around to Mata Hari sooner or later."

"What's that?" The General pounced. "Do you know her?"

"No. No." Gerry hastily declined the honour. "Behaving oddly, was she? Most women do."

Poor Adele. It occurred to me that not the least of Tyler Meredith's charm in her eyes might have been that, having stolen his partner's wife, he would have had to move her to different premises. Whether or not the partnership was dissolved, he could hardly maintain her in his resident flat. A desperate woman might do a lot to escape this booby hatch, especially if she had been trapped here for any length of time. No wonder she was behaving oddly. The wonder was that anyone so odd as the General himself was able to register it.

The General was still regarding us expectantly, but we let the silence drag on. Perhaps it's cynicism, or perhaps it's a natural consequence of being in PR, but we've found that people seldom confide in you without actually expecting you to *do* something about the situation.

We waited for the crunch. It wasn't long in coming, delivered more in sorrow than in anger, as though he has expected better from us. We weren't shaping up as the fighting force an ambitious General had the right to anticipate leading.

"What are we going to do about it, eh?" He paused only fractionally, as though suspecting he wasn't going to get an answer from us. At least, not a useful one.

"I'll tell you. We'll set a trap. Catch her in the act. And then we can deal with the little traitor."

How far was one expected to go in humouring a client's relatives? A grotesque vision of a blindfolded Adele facing a firing squad rose up before my eyes. I balked at visualizing the possible members of the firing squad. That would be above and beyond the call of duty, and besides, Zayle seemed quite fond of his wife for some obscure reason. Humouring his father to that extent wouldn't gain us any gratitude.

Unlike me, Pandora was soothed by the flow of conversation. She was a companionable little cat and very fond of social gatherings. The new human on her horizon was worth investigating. She dropped to the floor, stretched luxuriously, and strolled over to the General.

"What we'll do . . ." the General continued. It was easy to see that there was going to be no nonsense about asking for volunteers this time. We were being given our orders and that was that.

"Prrow?" Pandora was not accustomed to being ignored when she chose to exert her charms. She reared up, placing both front paws on the General's knee. "Prrow?"

"Eh?" Momentarily diverted, the General looked down at her, and then accusingly at me, as though what might have been reasonably expected to be a secure piece of my clothing had come adrift.

"Pandora," I called. "Come here."

"Pandora," the General said thoughtfully, making no response to her overtures. "A bit on the thin side, isn't she?"

"I think she's just built that way," I said defensively. "She eats like a horse."

"Perhaps she'll fatten up." The General leaned down and prodded a tentative forefinger into her ribs.

"Pandora, come back," I said. "Don't bother the General. He doesn't like cats."

"Nonsense!" the General boomed. "Of course I like cats. We often had them in the front lines." He prodded Pandora again. "Quite tasty, they were."

Pandora flinched away from the prodding finger and backed toward me, a thoughtful light in the eyes she kept fixed warily on the General. She backed until she bumped into my ankles, then, with an "Aaar-ahh!" she whirled and scrambled for my shoulders. She seemed to feel that she was adequately protected when she placed my neck between herself and the rest of the world.

The General frowned at her judiciously. "Keep at her," he said. "Fatten her up properly and she'll do you two or three days."

Beside me, I heard Gerry gag quietly, but I was too stunned to do more than murmur, "Yes, sir." The General's notion that I was packing Pandora as some kind of emergency rations was too mind-boggling to be taken in. I resolved I wasn't going to let her out of my sight while we were in this house. And if the General made one false move toward Pandora, I'd break his arm even if I was court-martialed for it.

"We'll deploy our forces." Dismissing the subject of Pandora and serenely oblivious to our reactions, the General went back to his strategy. "Use our men to the best advantage." He frowned. "It's a nuisance Geoffrey isn't here—I was counting on his help."

I was wishing he were here myself. With the General in this mood, I felt our side needed all the reinforcements it could get.

"He may be on his way." Gerry stood up hopefully. "Perhaps, if I went and looked for him—"

"Sit down!" The General could recognize a shirker when he saw one, and Gerry wasn't going to get out of it this time.

"It was just a suggestion." Gerry smiled weakly, relapsing into his seat.

"Now, you"—the General indicated me—"will take sentry duty on this floor and the floor below. Patrol the entire area—but keep out of sight."

"Yes, sir," I said, trying to figure out the mechanics of that one.

"You"—he glared at Gerry with distaste—"will have to take the upper floors—and the roof."

"Aye, aye, sir," Gerry said, getting his Services rather unfortunately muddled.

"I'll take the ground floor myself." The General frowned again. "I wish Geoffrey were here—he's the only man I'd trust on the back exit."

Pandora rumbled something low in her throat. The General glared at her, but obviously realized the impracticability of trying to discipline a cat for insubordination.

"You're sure you're perfectly clear as to your duties?" he queried.

Gerry and I nodded dumbly. We were as clear as we'd ever be.

"Very well." The General stood up. "Let's get to it!"

Chapter 14

Penny was just emerging from the surgery as we marched downstairs to station me at my post. I thought there was a slightly strained air about her. The General simply nodded to her brusquely, then swept Gerry back up the stairs, presumably to install him—and perhaps drill him in his duties—before taking up his own post in the lower regions.

Oddly, Penny didn't nod back—nor did she speak to any of us. She moved toward the stairs as though oblivious to us all. It wasn't like her. I moved forward and intercepted her, forcing her to look at me.

"Penny," I said. "Are you all right?"

She looked at and through me. "Yes," she said vaguely.

"We came as soon as we could after you telephoned. I'm sorry, but we got waylaid by the General. We were here in the house, at least, if you needed us. Don't be angry—" I broke off. There was no anger there. In fact, there seemed to be nothing at all there—not even Penny. I began to get worried. More worried, that is.

"Penny, what's wrong?"

"I want a breath of air." She tried to move past me. "I must go for a walk. A long walk."

"Penny!" I caught her arm, pulling her back. "Penny, what's the matter?"

"I must go for a walk," she repeated. "I must have air."

"Penny—" Cold panic seized me. "You haven't been sniffing that new anaesthetic, have you?"

She looked at me blankly. "I must go for—"

"All right, all right. I heard you the first time. Penny, just tell me this. What frightened you? Why did you telephone?"

"Telephone?" It might never have been invented. She said the word as blankly as though she were living in as distant a world as those the General inhabited. For an unsettling moment, I wondered if it were catching. Then I pulled myself together.

"Penny!—PENNY!" It was ridiculous to shout at her, still more ridiculous to want to shake her. I had her gaze on me, but I didn't have her attention. I couldn't even begin to guess where that might be focused. "Penny—"

"I must go for a walk," she repeated mechanically. "I must have air."

"At least, put your coat on." I capitulated, letting go of her arm. "It's getting cold outside." Perhaps, after she had had her walk, she would be more herself. Pandora shifted on my shoulder and grumbled restlessly. She didn't like it, either.

"I must have air." Still unseeing, probably unhearing, for she made no move to get her coat, Penny began to descend the stairs. "I must go for a long, long walk...." Her voice trailed away.

Must. It was an unlikely word to keep using. Perhaps that was what made me uneasy. I stared after her retreating figure. Should I let her go, or should I—

"You're not on guard!" The General's crisp complaint whirled me about to face him. "I came down those stairs, not trying to be quiet—practically stamping my feet—and you don't even glance my way. Fine sentry! The enemy could slip up behind you and slit your throat and you wouldn't know a thing."

And *that* was just the sort of cheery thought for the night that I needed right now. I wondered if the General had ever heard the word "morale"—or whether he thought it didn't apply to the troops under his command.

"Yes, sir. Sorry, sir," I muttered. Pandora added a couple of embellishments of her own to my remarks, but the General ignored us both. The lower ranks weren't supposed to have feelings—only duties.

He pulled himself up, drew a deep breath, and I was obviously about to get a practical demonstration of the technique that had made him the terror of the troops when the front door slammed. He instantly forgot me and turned toward the stairs. "Is that you, Geoffrey?"

I was right behind him. It wasn't like Penny to slam doors. Unless the wind had wrenched it out of her fingers and slammed it shut. But there had been no wind when we came in.

"Geoffrey?" There was no answer; the hall was dark and silent below us. "Geoffrey?"

"I think it was Penny going out," I said.

"Late." The General glanced at his watch. "Very late. I can't understand what's keeping him."

"The conference, sir," I reminded him. "Very important. At the War Office, I think." With a sinking feeling, I wondered if I was going to have to keep reminding him all night. How firm was his grasp on anything he was told?

"War Office!" The General snorted. "War Office! They—" He glanced at me sharply and bit back whatever else he was going to say. Obviously, officers kept their worst opinions of their colleagues from the lower ranks.

"Nevertheless," he continued pettishly, "Geoffrey *ought* to get here as soon as possible. I particularly impressed upon him how urgent it was. Vital to the war effort. A matter of national concern. Life and death."

"He'll break away as soon as he can, I'm certain."
I wondered if Sir Geoffrey was in the telephone
directory. It might be a good idea to nip into the living quarters and warn him that he was expected to
rally round, present arms, and play hunt-the-spy.
On the other hand, perhaps he was weary of these
alarms and excursions and might more kindly be
left to port and cigars by his own hearth. The
General, I had already noticed, expected rather a lot
from his friends.

"Quite right," the General said. "True-blue,
Geoffrey. Never shirks his duty. He'll be along."

Down below, the front door slammed again. I
beat the General to the top of the stairs. "Penny?" I
called. "Is that you?"

"No." The voice was too deep for Penny and
there was a military precision to the footsteps march-
ing across the hallway as though in time to martial
music.

"Gone missing, has she?" Sir Geoffrey mounted
the stairs at double time. I spared a moment to hope
I had that much energy at that age. I doubted it,
though. I hadn't *that* much energy at *this* age.
Obviously, the military was a healthier life than public relations. *Any* life must be a healthier life than
public relations.

"Lost her, have you?" Sir Geoffrey pulled up in
front of me, eyes sparkling, not even breathing
deeply, ready for any adventures the night might
bring.

"No, nothing like that," I protested feebly, wondering how I could resign my share in any adventure

to him—he was far better able to cope with it. "She just stepped out for a breath of air, that's all. I just wondered if she—"

"That's the little girl you've had helping Endicott?"

I nodded. Penny wouldn't have relished being described as a "little girl," but to Sir Geoffrey, anyone under forty was obviously a babe-in-arms.

"Saw her as I came along the street," he informed me. "Didn't look too well." He frowned professionally. "Seemed almost in a daze. Spoke to her, but she looked right through me." He brightened. "She might not have recognized me and thought I was trying to pick her up."

"No time for that, Geoffrey." General Sir Malcolm advanced upon us. "She's not the one we've got to worry about. This was going on before she appeared on the scene."

"Eh?" Sir Geoffrey swung his alert attention to his friend. "What was?"

"Back to your post!" the General thundered at me. I backed up smartly. Pandora, who hates loud noises, made a suitable comment for both of us.

"Come downstairs." He turned back to Sir Geoffrey. "You're the only man I'd trust to cover the back exit tonight. I'll fill you in on the way."

They descended the stairs and I told myself I wasn't interested in these newest figments of the General's imagination, anyway. Let them have their secrets. The only problem was that I was stuck on guard here, with no clear idea of whom—or what—I should be guarding against. I wondered how Gerry was making out.

The mutter of voices died away downstairs, leaving the house more silent than ever. Pandora began to purr; that suited her to a T.

"It's all very well for you," I told her. "No worries, no work to do, no problems, spoiled within an inch of your life . . ."

"Prrryeh," she agreed, slithering down into my arms to blink up at me contentedly.

The front door opened and shut again. Was it the General going out, Sir Geoffrey abandoning his post, or—I moved to the top of the stairs again. "Penny?"

"What's that?" Inspector Rennolds came into view. "You still here?"

"Not still," I corrected, "again. I came back later." I'd forgotten we'd arranged that late appointment for him. Surely, Penny ought to be back to resume her nursing duties—she wouldn't have forgotten, she took things like that seriously. On the other hand, she'd said she wanted to take a *long* walk.

"Oh!" Just short of the top of the stairs, Rennolds halted. "You've got that cat with you."

"Prryeh." Pandora regarded him thoughtfully. He didn't stamp his feet and he wasn't shouting. She yawned at him with sleepy approval.

"She seems different." Hesitantly, he resumed his progress, drawing even with us. "Friendlier."

"You didn't meet her at her best," I reminded him. "She was very upset at that show."

Pandora's homely purr throbbed loudly in the

stillness. Rennolds advanced cautiously, a man determined not to be disarmed.

"You can pat her," I said. "She won't mind."

"No, no." He shied away, a touch of his old phobia showing. "No time. I'm late for my appointment now." He glanced toward the surgery door anxiously. "The dentist hasn't given up on me, has he?" he asked hopefully. "I'm quite late. It couldn't be helped."

"I'm sure he wouldn't cancel *your* appointment," I said.

He looked as though he'd been afraid of that. For someone who'd been so anxious to get an appointment this afternoon, he was dragging his heels just like the rest of us now that the hour was actually in view.

"The case is coming along quite well." He offered the information as though it might bring him some reward—like the miraculous cure of an aching tooth without the necessity of going through any unpleasant mechanics. "We expect developments soon. Possibly an arrest within forty-eight hours."

He sounded like an official press release. I wondered if he remembered that I was in that business myself, or whether he was mistaking me for a reporter.

"That's fine," I applauded. "Congratulations. But the dentist is waiting."

"I'm aware of that." He was annoyed, perhaps disappointed. Had he been expecting me to try to pump him for further information? If so, he was going to stay disappointed. I didn't particularly care who had done the murders so long as it wasn't my client. And I would be delighted to get the whole thing over with so that I could stop holding Zayle's hand, riding herd on his wife, and playing soldiers with his father. I wanted to get back to the paying clients again.

If Zayle *was* the killer, I didn't want to know that, either. Not to the point of angling for advance information. The blow would fall soon enough, in that case, and I'd just as soon find out when the rest of the populace did.

"You might be surprised, you know," he said.

"Nothing surprises me," I said. "Least of all, delaying tactics at the dentist's."

He drew himself up and gave me an *et tu, Brute* look, although we'd never been on those terms to begin with.

"All right," he said with the sort of hauteur Pandora would use if she could talk. "I'm going."

He didn't go in any hurry. He seemed to be hoping I might change my mind and call him back for a nice long gossip. I didn't.

Pandora stirred uneasily as the strong whiff of antiseptic eddied out at the opening of the surgery door. I soothed her. She was really fairly relaxed. She seemed to realize that, this time, those strange smells had nothing to do with her. She nestled into a slightly more comfortable position in my arms and went back to sleep.

I went back to patrolling the empty hallways, up the stairs and down again. Now that Rennolds was gone, I missed him. And all this pacing lent itself too readily to an accompanying brooding. I wondered if the General would notice my absence if I sneaked up another flight and visited Gerry. I doubted that he was enjoying his sentry-go either, and he didn't even have a sleeping Pandora for company.

I stopped pacing and listened. There was no sound from below, nor from above. You couldn't even hear anything stirring in the surgery. They don't build houses like that anymore. Probably just as well. There's nothing like total silence for undermining one's nerves.

Why was it so quiet downstairs? Had the General suddenly slipped into one of his lucid intervals, aware of the correct time and place, and been persuaded by Sir Geoffrey to roam round to the pub?

And why was it so quiet upstairs? It was most unlike Gerry. Failing anything else to trip over, he could usually manage to fall over his own feet.

And why the silence from the surgery? Not that I expected Rennolds to be anything but stoic when faced with the drill, but—

My mind refused to play anymore. All this was simply masking my real worry. The one I didn't want to face. Where was Penny?

I thought I heard a movement, too quiet to be anything but stealthy, downstairs. I moved swiftly to the head of the stairs, peering down, unable to distinguish anything in the darkness below.

"Penny?" I called softly, but without any real hope.

I should never have let her go. No matter how much she insisted. At least, I should have made sure she put her coat on first. She wasn't herself. Even Sir Geoffrey had remarked on it.

Why hadn't Sir Geoffrey caught her and brought her back? He was a doctor, wasn't he? He ought to have recognized she was in no fit condition to go roaming the streets by herself. What kind of a quack was he?

But my mind wouldn't let me get away with placing the blame on anyone else. Penny was my responsibility. She was in this because we had asked her to substitute for Zayle's flu-bedded nurse. She had even stayed late tonight because of the late appointment with Rennolds I had arranged.

So why wasn't she here for it? Why had she dashed out on the feeble excuse of needing air? There was more to it than there seemed. Why had she kept using such a curious word as *must*? She *must* go for a long walk. There was nothing obligatory about going for a walk. She could have got quite enough fresh air standing on the doorstep.

Distracted though I had been by General Sir Malcolm, I should have been more quick-witted. I should never have let her go. And—there was something else disturbing. What was it? I grappled with recollections of the last hour or so, and then I had it.

Sir Geoffrey's snap diagnosis of Penny. "*Seemed almost in a daze.*" Now that I thought about it, that was the way she had appeared to me, as well. The way she didn't quite focus, the way she kept repeating words.

A daze—or a state of shock.

A state of shock. That fitted Penny's condition better than any other explanation. She had come rushing out of that surgery incoherent and desperate to escape to the outside world.

What had happened in that surgery?

What was happening in there now? What had Rennolds walked into?

I was at the door, turning the handle noiselessly. The door swung inward silently and I slipped just inside, so quietly that no one was aware of my presence.

I promptly went into a state of shock myself.

Endicott Zayle had gone raving mad.

Chapter 15

It was worse than I had feared. A nightmare scene far beyond anything a decent, reticent nightmare had ever produced in the haunted, broken hours just before dawn.

Rennolds slumped in the dental chair, oblivious to everything taking place. Above him, the dentist crouched purposefully, more reminiscent of the Demon Barber of Fleet Street than an honest Harley Street practitioner.

The aura of evil hovered in the air as the dentist's drill—armed with the thickest, largest burr, descended toward the unknowing Rennolds.

For the scene was grotesquely askew: Rennolds was not leaning back against the headrest with his mouth open; the dentist was not concentrating on a discoloured cavity.

Rennolds was slumped forward.

His forehead rested against the porcelain tray of instruments; the vulnerable nape of his neck was exposed to the descending drill.

Zayle was insane; he had to be. There was a mindless vindictiveness about the act that went beyond revenge—beyond sanity. His figure was almost totally enshrouded by the long white jacket. The surgeon's cap covered his hair and was pulled low on his forehead. The surgical mask covered the lower half of his face and partially protected his neck. There wasn't much exposed surface from which he would have to wash the bloodstains before departing.

He leaned forward, concentrating almost lovingly on the target area. His small, well-shaped hand brushed the indentation at the base of the skull as though testing for the most vulnerable spot. His thumb found it, pointed fingernail digging into it, and the humming drill began its slow descent.

There was nothing I could do. I stood there, fighting that grim knowledge. At this stage, trying to rush Zayle was useless.

In another few seconds, the drill would bite deep into that warm, throbbing, mortal flesh. Blood would spurt, and bits of bone and soft gray brain itself would splatter through the room, staining walls, ceiling, and linoleum.

It was good-bye to Inspector Rennolds. There was no way I could reach him in time.

Unless—

The sudden inspiration leaped into my mind and seemed to crackle in the very air like electricity.

Pandora caught it. She woke abruptly, raising her head to glare at me with bright blue eyes, the pupils of which had narrowed to suspicious slits.

Sorry, old girl, I apologized to her mentally—and hurled her across the room at the dentist.

She landed, clawing and spitting, between his shoulder blades, digging for a foothold.

The drill flew backward from his nerveless hand. Once more, he emitted that curiously high-pitched scream and reeled back, both hands raking desperately behind him to try to dislodge the snarling fury that had attacked him.

I was across the room in three strides, no longer worried about how much noise I made.

Pandora leaped clear as I grasped the dentist's shoulder and spun him into position for a knockout blow.

Then, just too late to pull my punch, out of the corner of my eye, I saw Zayle. He was lying, curled into foetal position, in the far corner of the room, a peaceful smile on his face.

My fist cracked into the fragile jaw with full ferocity. As she crumpled to the ground, the surgeon's cap fell from her head and a dark cascade of curls spilled across the linoleum as she hit the floor.

I stood there, staring down at her in dazed horror. It wasn't possible. Why should she—?

The house was suddenly filled with the sound of

running footsteps. From all directions, they converged on the surgery.

Sir Geoffrey rushed to the dental chair, checked Rennolds's pulse, nodded with relief, and began giving first aid.

Adele rushed to Endicott Zayle, calling his name in tones more anxious than I would have expected.

Gerry came up behind me. "Are you all right?" he asked. Pandora marched up to him for comfort, uttering bitter complaints about the treatment she had received, demanding his sympathy and attention.

General Sir Malcolm stooped and snatched the surgical mask from the face of the limp figure on the floor and straightened up, beaming with satisfaction.

"Good lad," he said approvingly. "You've nabbed the traitorous little wench!"

First things first. While the others administered first aid to the stricken and waited for the police to arrive to deal with Morgana Fane, Gerry and I went looking for Penny.

We split up outside to quarter the area. Gerry went toward Wigmore Street and I struck off toward the next most likely section.

I found her walking up and down Marylebone High Street. She didn't seem to recognize me, but I was prepared for that. This time I knew the reason why.

"Penny." I caught her arm gently and halted her aimless progress. "Penny?"

"I need air." She tried to pull away. "I must go for a long walk."

"Penny." I was saddened, but not surprised. I

had been listening before I left the house, and I had also seen Morgana Fane in action, without knowing it at the time. I knew what had to be done.

"Penny!" I thrust my hand in front of her face and snapped my fingers sharply. "Come out of it!"

"Wha—?" Dazedly, she shook her head, looking around us with bewilderment. "Where are we? What are we doing here?"

"We got caught up in a bad dream," I said. "But we're all right now."

She began shivering and I held out her coat, which I had brought along. Gerry had borrowed a coat of Adele's in case he was the one to find her.

"I don't understand—" She pulled the coat on gratefully. "I can't remember—" Wrinkling her forehead, she tried. "I was in the surgery. I had to stay late because Miss Fane was coming for an appointment—"

Of course that was the reason she would have had to stay late. Doctors and dentists have to protect themselves against possible accusations of sexual misdemeanours which might be brought by female patients—either hysterical or opportunistic—who find themselves alone with a hapless male. That's why a nurse has to be present. That was why Penny had to work late. Not because of Rennolds's appointment, but because Morgana Fane was coming back.

"I don't understand it all myself," I said, "but I'm beginning to. Let's get back to the surgery and find out what else has been going on."

•   •   •

I was glad that Morgana Fane had been taken away by the time we returned. The rest of them gathered in the Zayle living quarters.

Rennolds was still among them, seemingly untouched by his close miss with a sticky fate, if you discounted the spasmodic shudders that shook his whole body at regular intervals. His colleagues had obviously taken one look at him and decided they could wait until morning for his statement. Meanwhile, Sir Geoffrey was making sure the inspector was quietly getting basic treatment for shock. He'd been given a seat so near to the fire that his suit would have been smouldering if he'd been an inch closer; Adele spooned enough sugar into his cup of tea to turn it into syrup; we were all letting him ramble on—the theory being that talking about it helps.

But he was in a bad way still. He didn't even seem to notice that Pandora—to score me off—was lying in his lap. He was even stroking her absently—that was the real measure of his condition. In the ordinary way, he'd have shooed her off. Rather, he'd never have let her get near him to begin with.

"There'd been that early publicity—forgotten over the years," he was saying, "about her having been discovered in a seaside holiday show. But no one ever went too deeply into just what her act was. It didn't take much digging, once we'd started, to uncover that she and her partner did a sort of magic act, leaning more on a combination of hypnosis and mind reading than on actual magic."

"Damned silly wench!" the General snorted. "Kept waving some sort of medallion under my nose and insisting we'd been playing chess for hours.

Knew perfectly well that she'd only just come into the room."

I spared a moment of silent compassion for Morgana Fane. Hypnotizing a subject who hopscotched the decades must have led to nightmares. The posthypnotic suggestion only worked sporadically when the General considered himself in the 1914 era he'd been in when she hypnotized him. Whenever he time-traveled to another favourite era, most of what had happened in the previous era was forgotten—or remembered too well. No wonder Morgana had been so upset when the General recently demanded an introduction to her. She had seen her alibi for the time of Tyler Meredith's death slipping into the oblivion of an old man's memories. Until that moment, she had not realized how precarious the General's grasp of reality might be. Or how it might affect her plans.

"Did she expect to get away with it?" That was a good question, coming from Endicott Zayle. He was such a perfect subject for hypnosis that staring into Pandora's eyes had practically sent him into another trance. At the faintest murmur of a posthypnotic suggestion from Morgana Fane, he'd have started down Oxford Street starkers and on all fours. Except that she'd undoubtedly had a more sinister fate planned for him.

"The weight of circumstantial evidence would have been against *you*." Rennolds shuddered abruptly again. "She'd have redressed you in the bloodstained clothing and you'd have been found there with me—with my body."

Pandora stirred and complained. She hadn't bargained for earthquakes when she climbed into that sheltering lap.

"She'd probably have convinced you that you'd done it," I told Endicott Zayle, remembering bitterly the struggles I'd been through because his mind had seized upon the notion that I needed emergency treatment. I must have said the wrong thing to him somewhere along the line, since he'd come out of that trance with the firm impression that our cover story was genuine.

"Nonsense!" His eyes flicked guiltily around the room. "I'm not that weak-minded."

"She convinced you that she was lying dead in your dental chair and got you out of the way so that she could murder your partner," I reminded him. But even though she had planted firmly in his mind the command that he must not go near the police, she had not been able to quell the sense of self-preservation that had sent him scurrying to his public relations men to put the best face on his hallucinatory problem. Perhaps Endicott Zayle might not have come out of it so badly after all.

"At worst, she'd have had you babbling a confession as soon as you surfaced." Rennolds was in no doubt about the lady's ability. "At best, she'd have shaken your confidence to the point where you'd wonder if you really had killed me in a moment of mental aberration. And if you weren't sure and were behaving suspiciously, it might throw the boys off the scent. At least, sidetrack them until she'd had time to clear out of the country. There are still places in the world where extradition treaties are nonexistent."

"Why?" Adele demanded. "Why should she want

to kill Tyler Meredith?" The Honourable Edytha
had been killed, too, but that wasn't going to concern
Adele.

"Ah," Rennolds said. "Once you saw those early
handbills for the act, it was all clear. Some of them
had pictures. Her partner in the act was Tyler
Meredith. In fact, once we knew where to look and
what to look for, we found the record of the marriage."

"You know," Gerry said, "that explains something that was puzzling me. Meredith seemed to
spend most of his time getting engaged—'on spec,' as
it were—to females with money and/or influence.
And yet he never seemed to have tried it on with a
famous model like Morgana Fane. It wasn't natural—
not for him."

"Her own marriage was to have taken place
next week. That means"—I was on the trail of the
indictable offence—"that she wouldn't have been
legally married to her Lord—not with Tyler
Meredith still alive. Unless—"

"No," Rennolds said. "There'd been no divorce.
It would have been bigamy."

"And Tyler Meredith was planning to be a
bigamist, too." Gerry paused to contemplate such
awesome amorality. "They must have been a charm-
ing couple in the days when they were still together."

"Meredith was planning to try to sort out his
position," Rennolds admitted grudgingly. "That was
what set it all off. He was serious about a career in
politics—he couldn't go into Parliament with a time
bomb like that ticking away in his background. It
might be discovered as soon as any journalist wanted

an in-depth interview and did his homework properly. He wanted a divorce."

"But if *he* applied for a divorce now"—I saw the flaw in that—"after his wife married again, it would mean branding Morgana Fane as a bigamist. And she's had a hard enough time landing her Title. Once the Title discovered she'd been playing him for such a sucker, she wouldn't have had a hope in hell of getting him in front of the Registrar a second time."

"Precisely." Rennolds nodded, and shuddered violently again. "She had to stop Tyler Meredith—and anyone else who got in her way."

Pandora sat up in his lap and gave him her sharp opinion of people who couldn't keep still. He looked down at her in amazement, seeming to notice for the first time that she was there. And that his hand was actually stroking her. He jerked his hand away quickly and stared at her. After a moment, he replaced his hand and looked across at me.

"They tell me she saved my life," he said.

"We saw that drill coming down on you and she *flew* to the rescue," I said, maintaining strict accuracy while allowing him to form a slightly different picture of events than had actually been the case.

"Clever little thing," he admitted, stroking her with more enthusiasm.

Pandora grumbled the feline equivalent of *Watch it, buster,* and settled down again.

"Kept telling me we'd been playing chess for hours." The General was grumbling, too. "Harping on it. Chess! Strange obsession. Knew there was something wrong with her then and there."

"And you were right, Malcolm," Sir Geoffrey agreed.

"*My* dental chair," Endicott Zayle brooded. To him, that was the unkindest cut of all. "She murdered two people in *my* dental chair."

"Tyler Meredith had kept the marriage certificate—and it became his death certificate," Rennolds said. "When the Honourable Edytha found it in his flat, it became her death certificate, as well. She knew too much then. Also"—a thoughtful shudder racked him—"I believe there was an element of jealousy there. Fane didn't want him herself, but she didn't like the idea of any other woman having him."

"Dog in the manger!" the General snorted, as though he knew all about them. I'll bet they could be quite tasty, too.

"She wasn't hunting for the formula for the new anaesthetic, then?" Gerry was still trying to catch up. "She knew he'd hidden the marriage certificate somewhere?"

"Hunting for the formula? Why should she want the formula?" Endicott Zayle bristled. "*I* have it—I've always had it. I did a great deal of the work on that formula." His eyes got that shifty look again. "It's as much mine as Meredith's."

So that was the way he was going to play it. He might as well. Morgana Fane wasn't going to have any interest in it. In any case, she couldn't inherit—there was some kind of law about not being allowed to profit from your own crime. No other next of kin had been turned up for Meredith, and I doubted if fiancées—particularly considering their number—

had any claim on an estate without a specific bequest in a will.

"Always pampering your patients, Endicott," his father snorted. "I warned you no good would come of it!"

Trying to work out the logic of this gave us all a few quiet moments. I noticed Adele was holding her husband's hand. At least that seemed to have sorted itself out. In terms of enlightened self-interest, they were quite well matched.

"I should have paid more attention to our local MP," I said, remembering her reference to Tyler and the stage, which I had misinterpreted. "She seemed to know more than anyone about the real position."

"She cleared up quite a lot for me," Rennolds said. "She knew he was trying to sort out an earlier marriage, but not the identity of the woman involved. I believe"—he looked thoughtful—"that all-night sitting in the House might have saved her life. It kept her away from the danger area here, and Fane had gone berserk towards the end." He took a quiet fit of shuddering—it would have looked like a malaria attack to anyone who didn't know.

Pandora was not prepared to make allowances. He'd had his last chance. She jumped to the floor in exasperation and looked around. She was still furious with me, she didn't trust anyone scented with antiseptic, and no one was paying any attention to her. It was a totally unsatisfactory situation. She went to ground behind Gerry's ankles and sulked.

"She kept appearing at such odd times," Endicott Zayle complained. "Anytime she had half an hour to spare, she popped in—as though I could do the necessary work on her in ten minutes."

"An excuse," Rennolds said. "She knew better than that. Meredith was a dental student when she married him. She knew her way around a dental surgery—and its instruments." Another shudder. "It let her come in and out when she could and she took the time to search the flat. Did she need that job done at all?"

"Just because it was cosmetic dentistry," Endicott Zayle said huffily, "that doesn't mean it was unnecessary. To someone in her profession, it was a matter of making the most of her assets. It's a shame," he reflected, "that we weren't able to get round to it. I don't suppose she'll want it done now."

"She has other problems on her mind," Rennolds agreed. "And it won't make any difference where she's going. You might," he added bitterly, "send her a reminder notice when they let her out in a few years."

"It won't make any difference then, either," Gerry said expertly. "She's the type that runs to fat. A few years of prison stodge will finish her."

Adele brightened perceptibly at that thought. It takes a woman to appreciate the full extent of such a prospect.

Penny yawned, Rennolds kept shuddering, and Endicott Zayle still looked fairly glassy-eyed. Whatever other explorations of the subject were to come, they could wait for another day. It was time to break up this party.

I looked across and signaled to Gerry. He nodded

and we both got to our feet. We hadn't time to say anything before Rennolds stood up gratefully.

"I'll drop you off," he said. "I've got my own car downstairs."

"Let *us* drop you." Gerry and I spoke in chorus. Even Endicott Zayle had abandoned contemplation of his own best interests long enough to flinch at the thought of Rennolds's getting behind a wheel in his condition.

"We're getting a taxi," I said. "We have to take Penny home, anyway. It won't be any more bother to take you. You can collect your car tomorrow. Er ..." Economy reared its head belatedly. "Where do you live?"

"Highgate," the inspector said. Penny lived in Wimbledon. We were still reeling when Sir Geoffrey intervened.

"I don't think I can allow that," he said.

"Really?" We tried to restrain ourselves from beaming at him.

"Quite right," General Sir Malcolm said. "We shall want to convene an inquiry first thing in the morning."

Rennolds paled. "Now, see here—"

"You'd never make it," Sir Geoffrey said. "Afraid I slipped a little medication into your tea. Don't want to be carried home, do you? Very hard to explain to the neighbours, a thing like that. Better stay the night here. There's a whole flat going spare."

"But—"

"Oh, I'll square it with your superiors first, if you like." Sir Geoffrey brought up the heavy guns. "Who d'you want me to ring—the Commissioner? The Home Secretary? The—"

"No, no." Rennolds collapsed back into his chair. "Perhaps you're right. I'll stay. I *don't* feel very well."

"We'll be getting along then," I said cheerfully. "It's been a pleasure to be your adjutant, Sir Geoffrey. If you ever decide to retire from medicine, you might think of giving PR a whirl. Perkins and Tate could use you."

"Think nothing of it," Sir Geoffrey said modestly.

Gerry was helping Penny on with her coat and I looked at Pandora. "Coming?" I asked.

Pandora seemed to be debating the point. She gave me a long, considering look.

A dog insists on making a hero out of his master. A cat is even more of a realist than a valet. A cat can face facts. She not only knows the truth, she makes sure that *you* know that she is coldly aware that she has thrown in her lot with a louse.

"I *said* I was sorry."

She considered a bit more.

"Please yourself," I said. "The rest of us are going home."

As I turned, the familiar weight suddenly hit my shoulder, and a wet nose nuzzled my ear.

"Prryehyow," Pandora said. I might be a louse, but I was *her* louse and she was sticking with me.

What would I want with a dog, anyway? It would be too much to try to live up to.

On my part, I had a sneaking suspicion that Pandora was not displeased at having been allowed—

positively encouraged—to get in a few licks of her own at the hated enemy in the white coat.

Live and let live. Neither of us was perfect.

We followed Penny and Gerry, and as the front door closed behind us all, Pandora nestled down on my shoulder and began purring contentedly. We were going home.

ABOUT THE AUTHOR

MARIAN BABSON is the author of more than twenty-five mysteries. Winner of the Poisoned Chalice and Sleuth awards, she was also a nominee for the British Gold and Silver Dagger awards. She is listed in *Publishers Weekly* as one of today's best British mystery writers. She lives in London.

Where Can YOU Get Murder, Mystery, Mayhem
And Enjoyment Altogether?

THE AGATHA CHRISTIE
MYSTERY COLLECTION!

Enjoy **AND THEN THERE WERE NONE** as your introductory novel in
The Agatha Christie Mystery Collection. Sample this novel for 15
days—RISK FREE! If you aren't satisfied, return it and owe nothing.
Keep **AND THEN THERE WERE NONE** and pay just $12.95 plus s&h
(and sales tax in NY & Canada). You will then receive a new volume
about once a month with the same RISK-FREE privilege!

FREE! **THE NEW BEDSIDE, BATHTUB & ARMCHAIR COMPAN-
ION TO AGATHA CHRISTIE** (a $12.95 value!!!) is yours to keep
FREE, just for previewing the first novel. You'll enjoy this 362-page
guide to Christie's World of Mystery.

EXCLUSIVE VALUE! These Collector's editions, bound in Sussex
blue simulated leather, are not sold in any bookstores!

Remember, there is no minimum number of books to buy, and you may
cancel at any time!

YES! Please send me **AND THEN THERE WERE NONE** to examine for
15 days RISK-FREE along with my FREE gift. I agree to the terms above.
Send to: THE AGATHA CHRISTIE COLLECTION
       P.O. Box 972
       Hicksville, NY 11802-0972

Mr/Ms._____

Address_____

City/State_____ Zip_____
Orders subject to approval. Prices subject to change.
Outside U.S., prices slightly higher.   41640   ACBBB